THE EXPLOSION OF THE RADIATOR HOSE

ALSO BY JEAN ROLIN IN ENGLISH TRANSLATION

Christians in Palestine

THE EXPLO- SION OF THE RA- DIATOR HOSE

(AND OTHER MISHAPS, ON A JOURNEY FROM PARIS TO KINSHASA)

a novel by jean rolin
translated by louise rogers lalaurie

DALKEY ARCHIVE PRESS
CHAMPAIGN AND LONDON

Originally published in French as *L'Explosion de la durite* by P.O.L éditeur, 2007
Copyright © 2007 by P.O.L éditeur
Translation copyright © 2011 by Louise Rogers Lalaurie
First edition, 2011

Library of Congress Cataloging-in-Publication Data

Rolin, Jean.
[Explosion de la durite. English]
The explosion of the radiator hose, and other mishaps, on a journey from Paris to Kinshasa
/ Jean Rolin ; translated by Louise Rogers Lalaurie. -- 1st ed.
    p. cm.
Originally published in French as: L'Explosion de la durite.
ISBN 978-1-56478-632-6 (pbk. : alk. paper)
1. Voyages and travels--Fiction. 2. Congo (Democratic Republic)--Fiction. I. Lalaurie,
Louise Rogers. II. Title.
PQ2678.O4153E8713 2011
843'.914--dc22
                        2010046196

Partially funded by the University of Illinois at Urbana-Champaign and by a grant from the
Illinois Arts Council, a state agency

Cet ouvrage a bénéficié du soutien des Programmes d'aide à la publication de Cultures-
france/Ministère français des affaires étrangères et européennes

Cet ouvrage, publié dans le cadre d'un programme d'aide à la publication, bénéficie du soutien financier du ministère des Affaires étrangères, du Service culturel de l'ambassade de
France aux Etats-Unis, ainsi que de l'appui de FACE (French American Cultural Exchange)

This work, published as part of a program of aid for publication, received support from
CulturesFrance and the French Ministry of Foreign Affairs

This work, published as part of a program providing publication assistance, received financial support from the French Ministry of Foreign Affairs, the Cultural Services of the French
Embassy in the United States and FACE (French American Cultural Exchange)

www.dalkeyarchive.com

Cover: design and composition by Danielle Dutton, illustration by Nicholas Motte; French
Voices Logo designed by Serge Bloch
Printed on permanent/durable acid-free paper and bound in the United States of America

When the radiator hose burst, the car had done exactly ninety-nine thousand four hundred meters, since its odometer was reset to zero. It was doing over one hundred kilometers per hour, with the needle on the temperature gauge stuck firmly in the red. Earlier, Patrice had stopped on two separate occasions to lift the hood and examine the engine, concluding from his observations that he would be able to carry on driving at the same speed.

A mistaken diagnosis, as easily demonstrated by the car's current condition, immobile on the side of the road, its windscreen splattered with boiling water, and twisters of steam rising from beneath the still-closed hood. With the hood up, the steam-twisters formed a dense cloud, and the radiator's remaining water gushed out as soon as the cap was unscrewed. For a few moments we stood—the three of us: Patrice, Nsele, and me—contemplating the disaster: the water gushing up in spurts like an intermittent hot geyser, and the thick rubber pipe, split along its entire length like a sizzling sausage bursting out of its skin. Then Nsele, a small, rather chubby man with a closely shaved head, began waving his arms up and down at the side of the road, sending distress signals to the passing traffic, as if it was perfectly normal in the Congo—or anywhere else, for that matter—to pull over out of the kindness of one's heart and help a motorist in distress. No doubt he would have had better luck waving a wad of money, but in the heat of the moment—and unusually for him—he hadn't thought to ask me for any, as yet. Discouraged by the indifference of the passing truck drivers, Nsele came over to suggest I call "Monsieur Kurt," who could send someone to get us out of there. I refused, objecting that Kurt wasn't running a charity or a towing service and that we had caused him enough trouble already. Preserving my good name, or what was left of it, in Kurt's eyes, was a matter even dearer to my heart than saving the car. And in any case, our low-lying position put my cell phone completely out of range. The incident had occurred on a narrow stretch of road sunk between two steep embankments of hard red clay, a feature that not only made it impossible to use my cell phone, but also prevented us from shifting the car any further away from the side of the road, so that it was doomed to continue blocking one of the lanes, leaving it vulnerable—if night fell before we could get it going again— to being hit from behind by a truck hurtling along at top speed. Patrice started to hunt for the toolbox and discovered that it had been stolen, along with the jack, apparently during the few days the car had spent parked in the secure port area, closed to public access. The tools wouldn't have been much help anyway. A heated disagreement followed between Patrice and Nsele, who tried hard to heap all the blame for the incident on his associate's shoulders, given that he was the only one among us with even a rudimentary grasp of mechanics, after which Patrice stationed himself in the middle of the road, waved down a truck, and negotiated the price of a ride to the nearest village. When he had gone, I found myself alone with Nsele, sitting inside the car while the temperature rose steadily, for what I predicted would be at least a three- or four-hour wait, during the course of which—inevitably—it was going to get very dark indeed.

While it was still light, Nsele affected a noticeably devil-may-care attitude, babbling happily that Patrice would soon be back with a new radiator hose—as if the nearest village was at all likely to boast an Audi dealership (for such was the make of our vehicle)—and that we would reach Kinshasa by nightfall. Hence he took no precautions whatever to ensure the car's safety, suggesting only that we might move it to the top of the adjacent slope, thereby getting ourselves out of the trap formed by the twin banks of clay. To do this, however, one of us would have to sit behind the steering wheel—or at least stand outside the car, next to the wheel, so as to be able to turn it—while the other pushed the Audi, which couldn't have weighed much less than a ton, up the slope. Nsele watched attentively while I struggled to pull up some of the bushes growing out of the embankment, or break off their branches to build some sort of barrier across the back of the car, large enough to alert the trucks arriving from behind and encourage them to alter their trajectory before they hit us. Then, he began wandering around like some earnest botanist, collecting grasses, which he gathered into slender bundles, placing them carefully on top of my construction. His reluctance to attack the bushes themselves was, I assumed, partly superstitious. The skeptic in me scoffed at the spirits that would soon come out to reclaim the bush; it was getting dark, and there was no hope of Patrice returning before nightfall. Nsele retorted that he wasn't afraid of spirits, but the military. He urged me to get back in the car and stay hidden, to avoid attracting the attention of passing army vehicles. For a challenge, and because I wanted to assess the full extent of our predicament, or perhaps just out of curiosity to see the landscape beyond the two embankments of clay, I climbed up the slope opposite. Reaching the top, I saw that we were indeed surrounded on all sides by the bush, or an area of apparently uncultivated land, with no one else in sight. A few low trees poked up here and there above the thorn bushes and tall grass, turned yellow by the drought. In the distance, I could see hillsides blackened by fire, some still glowing red. In broad daylight, this landscape would be devoid of grandeur. But it was not so now, in the low light of the setting sun, with a cacophony of calls emanating from the scrub—screeching, chirping, cooing, and a host of other noises, among which I made out the song of the yellowbill, like the hollow gulping of a bottle being emptied of its contents. In my new, elevated position I felt confident and strong, animated by a far greater sense of poetry than beforehand, down at the bottom of the rut, to which I would have to return all too soon. From a distance, even Nsele was restored in my sight as a pleasant, decent fellow. And to prove my complete indifference to the threat of passing soldiers, I called out to him in simple comradeship: "Cooo-eeee!" On the subject of spirits, there was one thing I noticed then, which I found disturbing: just after sundown, when the din from the bush was hushed for a moment, the dry grass began to crackle on either side of the road, just as if it was burning—burning with hellfire. Except that it wasn't burning at all—and not only that, but the stems remained perfectly still and upright; there wasn't a breath of air passing through them, so that when you looked closely, from above or below, it was impossible to make out even the tiniest movement, such as that of the insect, however minuscule, which might have been causing the noise. Yet the crackling persisted, almost deafening at times, and spreading all around me as I moved through the dry grasses standing motionless in the still air.

Night fell, and Nsele's mood darkened. He insisted I stay in the car from now on, and this time I complied, as I did when he asked me—for fear of snakes—to shut the one door I had been keeping slightly open. Half awake, Nsele plastered his smooth scalp with continuous applications of repellent that did nothing to deter the mosquitoes, while muttering endless recriminations against Patrice, pointing out that in his place, he—Nsele—would have been back ages ago with a new radiator hose purchased at the aforementioned Audi dealership in the next village. I was no more able to sleep than he. Every time a truck made itself heard in the distance, scraping its clutch at the top of the slope, I curled myself into a ball, waiting for the impact, and it seemed that when the glare of headlights flooded the road, bearing down on us at full speed, I somehow managed to make myself smaller still, recovering my normal size only when the truck overtook us in a cloud of dust, buffeting the car with an accompanying gust of air, the force of which testified to the narrowness of our escape. Despite my earlier, offhand reaction (only partly feigned) to Nsele's earlier warnings, the terror inspired in me by the threat of the military was in reality somewhat akin to that caused by the passing trucks. True, individual testimonies and press reports seemed to indicate (insofar as the latter could be given any credibility at all) that the military in these parts only murdered civilians on very rare occasions—and far less frequently than in the eastern part of the country. This reassuring thought did not, however, exclude the unpleasant possibility of being held for ransom, or beaten up. I was forced to acknowledge what a treat it would be for a Congolese soldier or policeman to get his hands—deep in the bush—on a white man liable to be prosecuted for spying, which I feared I had now become, in their eyes at least, following an incident just before disembarking at the port in Matadi.

Among the images of torture and humiliation that now presented themselves for my consideration, one stood out from all the others, for its detail and historical importance alike. The scene is from the personal Calvary of Patrice Lumumba, the ephemeral president of the Democratic Republic of the Congo in the months immediately following its birth: of all the heroes of African independence, Lumumba is arguably the only one to have retained his heroic status, as much for the circumstances of his demise as for the brevity of his reign (slightly less than three months), even though the latter bore the stain of a handful of massacres carried out under his authority, mostly against members of the Luba tribe, in the province of Kasai. I first came across the picture in a Soviet propaganda brochure with an orange cover, entitled *Patrice Lumumba and African Freedom*, as I was pleased to confirm on my return to France, when I found it again, against all expectations. The scene in the photograph had taken place some forty years earlier, and the photographer's name and background are not given (it was probably a still from the newsreel footage shown around the world at the time, which provoked a passing wave of indignation). Lumumba is seen with disheveled hair, minus his spectacles, his white short-sleeved shirt open halfway down his chest. The position of his left arm, pulled behind him, indicates that his hands have been tied behind his back. Of the three people visible in the photograph (apart from the soldiers standing in the background, with their backs turned) he is the only one looking straight at the camera, with an unfathomable expression possibly attributable to short-sightedness or a slight squint in one eye, but which might also signal despair and contempt in equal measure. The faces of his two companions, Okito and M'Polo, show naked terror. If the caption accompanying the photograph is to be believed, the scene occurred during Lumumba's transfer to the prison in Thysville (now called Mbanza-Ngungu). Prior to this—after his powers had been revoked by the President of the Republic, Joseph Kasavubu, in the early days of September 1960, and his detention under house arrest in Leopoldville (now Kinshasa)—Lumumba had managed to escape by car on the night of the twenty-seventh to the twenty-eighth of November, accompanied by his wife, one of his sons, and a few close associates. The circumstances of his escape are known—more or less, although they may have been altered or exaggerated—thanks to a number of eyewitness accounts including one from a certain "Jacques," quoted by the Soviet journalist Lev Volodine, in the brochure with the orange cover. "Jacques" had no doubt that Lumumba's plan was to reach Stanleyville (now Kisangani) where the population and authorities were largely favorable toward him, and which later became the crucible for a succession of uprisings against the authorities in Kinshasa and their Belgian or American allies, marked by atrocities that outraged Western opinion, particularly those perpetrated by the rebels against priests and nuns.

According to "Jacques," as quoted by Lev Volodine, who describes him as an "intimate associate of Lumumba," the fleeing prime minister's journey to the northeast attracted enthusiastic crowds whom he stopped to address several times with rousing speeches, losing valuable ground to the soldiers who had set off in his pursuit. After a last meal with his supporters and companions at Port-Franqui (now Ilebo), and a final oration at Mweka, Lumumba just managed to outdistance his pursuers, but was betrayed by a Belgian railway employee and captured as he was about to cross the Sankuru, a tributary of the Kasai River, beyond which nothing could have stopped him until he reached Stanleyville. More precisely, it seems that Lumumba and part of his retinue had left their vehicles, climbed into pirogues, and reached the opposite bank safe and sound, when the fleeing prime minister— possibly the victim of a trick, or concerned for the safety of his wife who had not yet made the crossing—paddled back across the Sankuru and fell into the hands of the soldiers. This episode took place at a village called Lodi, which I have been unable to find on the Michelin 1/400,000 map of central and southern Africa. From Port-Franqui—the nearest town to the unrecorded hamlet—Lumumba was taken to Leopoldville, where he spent the night at the Binza military camp. The next day, accompanied by Okito and M'Polo, he was taken by road to Thysville, and it is here that the scene photographed in the Soviet brochure with the orange cover seems to have taken place. Lumumba and his two companions were held for six weeks in Thysville, at Camp Hardy, before being taken out on January 17 and delivered into the hands of one Moïse Tshombé, the leader of the Katanga separatists, a protégé of the Belgian and U.S. governments (and the deposed prime minister's sworn enemy). Very little time elapsed between the departure from Thysville and Lumumba's assassination, in conditions that remain obscure, but which were plainly horrifying. From Thysville, Lumumba—still with Okito and M'Polo— was driven to Lukala where the three prisoners were taken aboard a plane bound for Muanda. According to some versions of the story, Lumumba agreed to leave Camp Hardy on the promise that his supporters would be waiting for him in Leopoldville, where he would form a new government. Instead of which, at Muanda, he was transferred aboard a DC-4, where a certain Lieutenant Zuzu was waiting for him with a handful of Luba soldiers from Kasai—members of the tribe massacred in the region around Bakwanga (now Mbuji-Mayi) by Lumumba's government troops. On the five-hour flight between Muanda and Elisabethville (now Lubumbashi), the capital of the breakaway province of Katanga, the prisoners were tied up together and subjected to a beating of such violence that it destabilized the plane and forced the Belgian crew to lock themselves into the cockpit to escape the horrific spectacle of this lynching. It seems that Godefroid Munongo, Tshombé's interior minister, travelled to Elisabethville Airport in person to take delivery of the prisoners. What happened next is widely disputed, but the report established in 1961 by a UN commission (which, it should be pointed out, was never allowed entry into the Congo), and later works such as the *Histoire générale du Congo*, published by the Congolese historian Isidore Ndaywel è Nziem in 1998, agree that Lumumba, Okito, and M'Polo were tortured—separately or together—in a villa near Elisabethville, before being killed in the same villa or by the side of the road near the village of Shilatembo. Moïse Tshombé and three of his ministers, including Munongo and two members of the Belgian military (one of whom was a colonel) were among the probable witnesses or perpetrators of the torture and executions. Ndaywel è Nziem confirms one version of the story, according to which the bodies of Lumumba and his two companions were buried and exhumed twice over before finally being dissolved in a bath of acid, under Munongo's supervision.

When I checked Ndaywel è Nziem's book in Kinshasa, and discovered that after being removed from Camp Hardy, Lumumba had been taken from Thysville to Lukala along the Matadi road, it occurred to me that his convoy might have passed by the very spot where the Audi remained stuck for several hours at nightfall. Had I known this at the time, the coincidence would have added an extra piquancy to my musings. But a careful look at detailed maps of the region shows that Lukala and Thysville (Mbanza-Ngungu) are respectively 133 and 184 kilometers from Matadi, so that in order to have broken down on the precise section of road taken by Lumumba's convoy on January 17, 1961, the Audi—forty-four years and eight months later—would have to have held out for at least another thirty-four kilometers before the explosion of the radiator hose.

It was in Leopoldville that I learned to drive, a few years before the death of Patrice Lumumba and, as it turned out, in vain, because I have used my skill only rarely since, and only when life saw fit to set me down in the presence of a Renault 4L. My driving hours— invariably at the wheel of a Renault 4L—probably amount to about a hundred in total, at least half of them on Congolese soil. My apprenticeship was confined at first to the intersection of Avenue Lilas and Avenue de Kalemie (both doubtless called something completely different back then) before progressing outwards in spreading, concentric circles to encompass the entire agglomeration of Leopoldville and its suburbs. After ten days I was able to drive without difficulty, on paved roads and dirt tracks alike, out to the site of the Kinsuka rapids on the Congo River, where Joseph Conrad almost lost his life and the manuscript of *Almayer's Folly: A Story of an Eastern River*.

The man who taught me to drive was named Bernard Lokole. He was my father's driver, and I remember giving him a watch, perhaps a somewhat inadequate reward for his services (it all depends on the quality of the watch). Under colonial rule—which he referred to, rather curiously, as "the Flemish times"—Lokole had served as a noncommissioned officer in the Force Publique, a kind of indigenous gendarmerie trained and commanded by the Belgians. In 1960, the year of the proclamation of independence, the Force Publique had mutinied and run amok here and there, pillaging and killing, reawakening the white population's atavistic terror of being torn limb from limb and having their homes razed to the ground by the very people who only the day before had served them with such apparent delight and dedication. Lokole may not have raped any nuns himself, but he probably dreamed of doing so when the troubles broke out, particularly since his generally affable character was susceptible to violent mood swings under the influence of drink or dope. The events to which I refer took place in 1965. It was probably in that same year—the year of my first sojourn in the Congo—that I bought the brochure *Patrice Lumumba and African Freedom* at the Globe bookshop, dedicated to the dissemination of Russian literature and Soviet propaganda. And what was the extent of my commitment to the cause of "African freedom"? What, indeed, was the extent of my commitment to anything at all, back then? I find it very hard, now, to determine why, at sixteen years of age, we adopt one ideological stance rather than any other. And how that stance can, over time, take on the character of a conviction, even a fanatical conviction, so that what began (at least in part) as an easy affectation, grows and hardens to become a more or less permanent, tyrannical framework shaping our entire existence.

In the summer of 1965, under the government of Evariste Kimba, the "done" thing among the youth of expatriate families was to gather in the afternoons by the pool at the Athénée, there to engage for the most part in long hours of diligent sexual maneuvering, feigning nonchalance, but in fact with very real, indeed fevered dedication. As a species, young expatriates were on the whole remarkable for their sporting prowess. I, on the other hand, was forced to compensate for my complete, debilitating inadequacy by the adoption of a radical (and, it must be said, paradoxical) political stance, enabling me to pass myself off with relatively little effort as an interesting intellectual, confident that on this score at least I would have no difficulty triumphing over my athletic young rivals, and that perhaps some of the American and Belgian girls I lusted after would be pleasantly surprised by my feats of eloquence. While the ideas I professed, in a continuous and doubtless exasperating stream of verbiage, were calculated to shock, the sparkling rhetorical form in which they were couched (and, on occasion, rendered completely undetectable) was liable to charm one or another of these girls sooner or later, because I was quite clearly taking such extraordinary pains solely for their own enjoyment—even while rubbing them the wrong way—and never once actually trying to win them over to the cause. Among the ideas that I embraced and expounded upon so wholeheartedly, drawing heavily on material from the Soviet brochure and other works of a similar persuasion, such as Frantz Fanon's *The Wretched of the Earth*, whose celebrated preface by Jean-Paul

Sartre urged indigenous peoples everywhere to murder citizens like the poolside habitués and myself (for as long as I shared their life and leisure hours, anyway)—among these ideas, some of which were passably entertaining and, I knew, capable of silencing the *jeunesse sportive* while at the same time highlighting their ignorance, not the least (besides my making excuses for Lumumba, whom everyone present took to be the devil incarnate) was the notion that the ruins of Great Zimbabwe bore comparison to the most famous monuments of ancient Egypt or Greece. This exercise brought other benefits than impressing girls, leading me to acquire a fair knowledge and favorable impression of African art, and to cultivate a genuine, unforced liking for the statuary of Benin or Ife, for example. But it is undeniable that in place of all that I would far rather have gotten laid.

The evening dances that occasionally prolonged these afternoons by the pool offered few opportunities for me to shine and plenty to display my shortcomings to the full. It was during one such evening, for reasons of protocol and certainly not mutual inclination, that I found myself dancing with the daughter of Joseph Kasavubu, the President of the Republic, the man who had overthrown Lumumba and delivered him to his henchmen, and who would himself, just a few months later, be removed from power by a coup d'état organized by Colonel Mobutu, whose movement Kasavubu had at first supported.

During this same period, unknown not only to the demographic attending these dances, but also to the world at large, Che Guevara was attempting to establish a guerilla base in the eastern Congo. Here he was confronted with the many difficulties recorded in his diaries, published long after his death, in terms rather similar to those used today by white businessmen eager to stigmatize the feckless negligence of their indigenous collaborators or subordinates. These same recriminations—over excesses, laziness, and bravado, ineptitude for organized combat, or the gratuitous cruelty of their Congolese partners—are all found, often rather more crudely put, in the accounts of the Cubans who fought alongside them, as collected in a volume published separately from the complete edition of Che's diaries (*The African Dream: The Diaries of the Revolutionary War in the Congo*, Grove Press, 2000). For his part, Guevara, who can't have done much preliminary reading before undertaking the trip, seems to have been particularly disconcerted by the Congolese *guerilleros'* systematic belief in *dawa*: an unction of holy water thought to liquefy enemy bullets in midflight, and to render combatants generally invulnerable, at least as long as they committed no infringement of the extremely strict rules regarding its use. Che also complained of Laurent-Désiré Kabila's distaste for combat zones, and his marked preference for hotels offering abundant supplies of whiskey and whores. He comforted himself with what were very probably delusions of another guerilla operation being led at the same time in Kwilu by Pierre Mulele, a man clearly far more courageous than Kabila, but who much later made the mistake of giving himself up to the Mobutu regime under pressure from his friends in Brazzaville, to be gratified on the evening of his return with a grand reception in his honor, after which he was handed over to the military the following morning and tortured to death. (In his aforementioned book, the historian Ndaywel è Nziem tells how

Pierre Mulele—every inch the model Marxist-Leninist—played on his troops' superstitions to impose iron discipline: taking care, for example, not to debunk a legend crediting him with the power of ubiquity, and the ability to turn himself into a snake—a legend so firmly believed by his men that whenever they encountered a reptile on a bush track, they would snap to attention and salute the creature with a hearty "Greetings, comrade!")

Among the reflections inspired by Guevara's sojourn in the Congo, one of the strangest, the most disconcerting with regard to the usefulness of revolutions in general, and the Congolese revolution in particular, concerns the condition of the peasantry: "What could the Liberation Army offer these peasants?" Che asked himself, in the epilogue to *The African Dream*. "That is the question which always bothered us." Because the peasantry, he added, at least in the region where he was attempting to set up his guerilla base, were not looking for agrarian reform, since they already owned the land or were free to use it as they pleased. Nor were they looking for credits to buy farm tools, "because the peasants ate what they tilled with their primitive instruments and the physical characteristics of the region did not lend themselves to credit-fueled expansion." Guevara concluded from this that in order to stimulate the peasantry's revolutionary ardor, he would have to create its nonexistent needs from scratch: "Ways would have to be found of fostering the need to acquire industrial goods," he wrote, seemingly unaware that he was reasoning in precisely the same terms as any representative of a multinational corporation, and never questioning the appropriateness of a revolution whose principal beneficiaries felt no necessity for it whatsoever.

Nonetheless, in 1965, revolutionary activity in the region was not confined to Che Guevara's fruitless endeavors. Two years earlier, a popular uprising, or something approximating one, had brought Alphonse Massemba-Debat (known as *le frère Alphonse*) to power in Brazzaville, on the opposite bank of the river from Leopoldville-Kinshasa. Several times a week, Brother Alphonse would appear on Brazzaville's television network, expounding at length before a crowd assembled more or less spontaneously for the occasion. And when I hadn't been commandeered for evening dance duty, I watched his broadcast speeches with fervent admiration, in the villa on the corner of Avenue Lilas and Avenue de Kalemie. And they were not, indeed, without merit. As I recall, Brother Alphonse sold the crowd nothing but empty promises and hot air, but he went about it with some talent: no overemphasis, sometimes an almost conversational tone, even the occasional touch of humor, giving an added poignancy to the invariably anxious, sorrowful expression on his long face, like a black Humphrey Bogart presiding over the fortunes of a momentarily socialist African republic, destined, as he had probably foreseen, to a dark and miserable fate (on March 25, 1977, Alphonse Massemba-Debat was executed by his peers after being implicated in the assassination of Marien Ngouabi, his successor as head of state).

In Leopoldville, and especially around my regular swimming pool, there was still much discussion of the events that had taken place a few months earlier in Stanleyville, where the rebels had once again seized power before being routed by a military intervention lead chiefly by the Belgians, with the Americans lending a hand. John McIntyre, officially the Commercial Counselor at the United States embassy, was reputed to be the CIA's head man in the Congo, and one of the architects of the operation. For reasons of protocol, and in spite of my father's paradoxically extreme, radical views—actually quite close to my own in that respect (or vice versa)—he was unable to shirk his duty to entertain McIntyre, nor could he help finding him far more fun than the Czech and Polish diplomats with whom he tried, largely unsuccessfully, to forge bonds of friendship. McIntyre exuded an aura of physical strength quite unusual for a diplomat, with pale, almond-shaped eyes, like a cat's. At least, that was the impression he made on me. Like all B-movie secret agents, he cut quite the figure in the dark suit he always wore to evening gatherings. He was a hard drinker, and this was doubtless one reason why my father liked him, despite their political differences, much as he tended to value any companion able to argue with him late into the night, with increasing rancor and confusion as the hours passed. These debates were generally staged around the bar of the villa on Avenue Kalemie, with its curving shape and shelves lined with bottles. I remember the bar all the more clearly because it was almost certainly there that I became blind drunk for the first time ever. Probably not in 1965, but the following year. Mobutu had seized power in the meantime, and would hold on to it for the next thirty-two years. The rebellion, or rebellions, were almost all routed, right across the country. Congo-Brazzaville advanced slowly on the path of socialism, and Brother Alphonse was still entertaining the crowds with his crazy ideas in television broadcasts that invariably ended with the anthem of the JMNR (*Jeunesse du Mouvement National de la Révolution*), whose lyrics exhorted the "imperialists" to "cease their clandestine bullying in our Congo." On the evening of a fine, relatively cool August day, doubtless spent as usual by the pool at the Athénée, the French ambassador's residence, almost opposite our villa on Avenue Kalemie, was the scene of a large reception in honor of two tyrants, Mobutu and Bokassa, the second of whom was also half insane. The ambassador's son was a friend of mine, and we watched the guests arrive—I think Bokassa wore a curious moleskin hat with a velvety sheen, and walked with the help of a white stick—before making off with several bottles of champagne to be drunk with the daughter of another diplomat, in the garden of our villa. Late in the evening, the ambassador's son taught us a drinking song ("Allons, la mère Gaspard!") which I can only remember singing on one other occasion in my life, three years later in 1969, not without some coercion, with a working-class family near Flins in Île-de-France, whom we were trying to convert to The Cause. After which I sank into a state of such drunkenness that I had to climb to my bedroom on all fours.

Roughly four hours went by before Patrice's return. He had found no Audi dealership in the nearest village, but had nonetheless retrieved an old piece of metal tubing, which he had had reforged to the dimensions of the burst radiator hose. With two rubber gaskets and a tube of extra-strong glue, working in the dim glow of a flashlight, he managed to secure the off-cut tube between the two orifices formerly connected by the radiator hose. He had also thought to equip himself with two bottles of Fanta—Nsele and I had had nothing to drink since the morning—and a yellow plastic jerrican containing twenty-five liters of water. Because connecting the engine to the radiator was not the only problem: the water in the radiator began to boil as furiously as ever, as soon as the engine was gunned. We removed the radiator cap completely to let the brew cool on contact with the air. Despite this, we had to stop about every ten kilometers to replace the water that had gone up in steam, and at longer intervals to fill up the jerrican. Even near the river, water is still a rare delicacy in the Congo, especially at night, and its price has to be negotiated with the supposed owner of its source. And all the while, the trucks that Patrice had overtaken earlier, frequently with no visibility, veering onto the sides of the road and threatening to bust the Audi's shock absorbers—these same trucks now overtook us in turn, and we were back where we had started. Overtaking the trucks required prolonged surges of acceleration during which the engine overheated and the water evaporated faster still, resulting in further, multiple stops. Last but not least, we had to contend with the tolls set up across the road by the military—sometimes official, sometimes spontaneous; in other words, improvised by solitary soldiers who would suddenly spring up out of the darkness. At each of these tolls, I was forced to hide as best I could on the back seat, to avoid (at best) the imposition of a special tariff. This exercise presented no particular difficulties: most of the roadblocks were badly lit, and the soldiers were content to hold out a hand to grab the small-denomination banknotes that Nsele had relieved me of earlier. Invariably, he or Patrice would hail the private with a "Good evening, Commander!" followed by an encouraging word, "Keep a good watch, now!" as soon as the banknote was pocketed. And in this way we could have transported a rocket launcher or a trunkful of hand grenades quite easily and without any fear of discovery.

At the halfway point, we stopped briefly in a small, noisy, dusty town where a large number of trucks were parked. It was quite cold by now, and with all four windows wound up, the glass was coated with condensation. We got back on the road, and by dawn we had reached a military-police barrier far bigger than the others, at which a huge number of bribes had to be distributed, and which remained closed throughout the night. The journey's final hours were spent in a state of such exhaustion and stupor that Patrice put all our lives at risk every time he tried to pass someone. Scrapings, clicks, and tappings of all kinds were now emanating from the car's various organs, and the bodywork, covered in mud and dust, looked ready to melt into the earthy landscape, bathed now in the pale light of the late dry season, through which we were passing in bad-tempered fits and starts. The radiator boiled, and the water ran out, incessantly. Given the difficulties I had experienced getting the car even this far, and the epic light in which I sought to cast the entire undertaking, my situation seemed to me—in my half-awake state—to be more and more like that of Hemingway's Old Man, watching the flesh shrivel gradually away from the body of his marlin. The isolated settlements through which we passed all gave the same impression of decrepitude and feverish activity, as if each was living in the expectation of something or someone that would never come. Every time a vehicle stopped, it was immediately surrounded by a crowd of vendors, petitioners, or rubberneckers, and it was clear that if we were finally forced to abandon the car in such circumstances, it would be stripped bare and reduced to a pile of spare parts. My anxiety and irritation increased as I sensed the complete indifference of my two Congolese associates, Patrice and Nsele, as to the car's ultimate fate, despite its supposed role in the future improvement of their lot (although, admittedly, I had not brought it here with that precise end in mind), and their far greater concern with the stashing of provisions of chikwangue and other bush products in the trunk. It actually occurred to me that they were incapable of envisaging the future and calculating accordingly, like most of the people I had encountered since my arrival in this country. This was self-centered reasoning, of course, taking no account of the years of war and disorder of various kinds from which the same country had barely begun to emerge, if at all, and which had left it completely prostrate.

The approach to Kinshasa, between hills shorn of their trees, restored Nsele's good spirits and his propensity for chatter. But he expressed himself chiefly in Lingala, to Patrice, so that I was unable to join in. Besides which, my entire consciousness, to say nothing of my body, was painfully and exclusively focused on a need to piss that had been growing stronger and more urgent for the past hour or two, and was rapidly approaching the moment when it could no longer be held in check. Even in the serenest of moods, it would have been difficult not to notice the air of dereliction swamping the capital, measurable, for example, in the state of the military camps, some of which, like Camp Kokolo, were so overwhelmed with filth that they resembled public garbage dumps. And yet it was often there, within those same perimeter walls, that the country's fate had been decided; there that the vocation of some of its leaders had been formed, while others had found themselves summarily dispatched.

Shortly before crossing the intersection where the Monument to the Martyrs of Independence stood unfinished (why suffer martyrdom, I thought, inappropriately, for so disappointing an outcome?), Nsele pointed out to me, on the right, the place of worship used by the church or sect to which he belonged—*la Manne ca-chée* or "Hidden Manna"—adding that it had been founded by a woman and that it was she who "preached." A bilingual argument ensued in Lingala and French, with Patrice, who maintained that the Bible denied women the right to preach. Nsele doubtless had a better idea than I of the Bible's exact pronouncements on this matter—although it seems likely that Patrice was right—and he distanced himself deliberately from the main topic to stress, according to his own reading of the Gospels, how much of a *bon vivant* Christ was, frequently engaging in unrestrained bouts of eating and drinking. I wondered which episode had led him to this conclusion—perhaps the wedding at Cana? With the debate in full swing we began the drive down Boulevard du 30 Juin, where fresh setbacks awaited us. But for now, as we turned onto this, the city's most majestic thoroughfare, I considered that I had achieved the first, the most difficult part of my plan, keeping the promise I had made to myself, my personal oath sworn the day I took delivery of the Audi on just the wrong side of the Paris beltway (the *périphérique*), in the southern suburb of Kremlin-Bicêtre.

The initial plan had been hatched two years earlier, by Foudron and myself, in the McDonald's at La Fourche—that celebrated parting of the ways on Paris's metro line 13—where he worked as a security guard. The scheme was intended first and foremost, and above all by Foudron himself, as a way of making money. Foudron had heard that in Kinshasa, a taxi could earn its owner over fifty dollars a day. Besides which, in Château-Rouge—a center for much Congolese business in Paris—he knew a man who ran a company specializing in the export of vehicles and assorted packages to Africa. After which several months went by with no further mention of the project, until a Congolese neighbor of Foudron's—a former noncommissioned officer with whom he maintained friendly relations—made him a gift of a secondhand car. The date must have been January or February, 2005. On April 1 of that same year, on the eve of the Pope's death, we set out to inspect the vehicle, which was parked on the curb—rather than alongside it—on a quiet street, bright with seasonal blossoms, in Vitry, a residential neighborhood of modest bungalows slightly further south of the *périphérique* than Kremlin-Bicêtre. The car in question was an old Opel Corsa that had apparently enjoyed a long sojourn in the open air with no maintenance whatever, to judge from its lusterless gray paintwork. Besides which, given its position on the Vitry-sur-Seine sidewalk, it was, we reasoned, in no fit state for the road. But a little farther down the same street stood a garage, which Foudron claimed to have contacted with a view to carrying out some basic servicing. Out of curiosity, I opened the front driver's side door and installed myself behind the steering wheel, noting that the space between this and the seatback—which was apparently locked in place—would accommodate only the puniest of drivers, and not only puny, but agile too. The weather was overcast and wet on this April 1, 2005, but the preceding days had been sunny, and the cockpit of the Corsa was pervaded by the faint, not unpleasant odor of jam given off by the materials used for the interior fittings of cars when they've been left to stew for extended periods of time. That evening, from a relative of Foudron, we obtained the details of a fellow Congolese by the name of Blondeau, who put us in touch with a business in the northern Paris suburb of Saint-Denis, specializing in the export of used vehicles. (This because the Château-Rouge contact had slammed the door in our faces once he realized a white man would be involved.) The negotiations were conducted by telephone, in Lingala, from a café next to the Paris regional electric rail (RER) station in Vitry. Here, Foudron talked at length about his declining health and sleepless nights, before evoking the distant day in Zaire when he had stopped smoking, after which he had gained the excess weight he now carried around. Given his height and build, both well above average, his corpulence had never constituted much of a handicap to his activities as a security guard, however, and may even have enhanced his dissuasive capacities. At 7:15 P.M., I climbed aboard the train bound for Paris, and Foudron stood for a while on the platform, a gigantic black-clad figure saluting me with a slow wave that conferred an unexpected air of solemnity on our parting.

And now here was Foudron, recumbent in Villejuif, another drab suburb forming the apex of an elongated triangle with Krelim-Bicêtre and Vitry-sur-Seine—recumbent more precisely on a bed in the Hôpital Paul-Brousse, hooked up to a drip, flat on his back, legs spread-eagled, the whole of the bottom part of his face covered with a breathing mask from which small puffs of steam escaped at regular intervals. With the metal window blind rolled three-quarters of the way down, the room was plunged in semidarkness. Yet no major health problem had declared itself before mid-April. On the eleventh of that month, we had travelled to Saint-Denis to make contact with an outfit by the name of World Transit, on Rue Charles-Michels, midway between the Seine and the tracks of the RER (line D). Leaving the station, we had taken the pedestrian underpass beneath the tracks, leading to a riverbank neighborhood that was now almost completely

Africanized. On Rue Charles-Michels, Foudron, complaining of a sharp pain in his right side, had walked "like a tortoise" (his own words), enjoining me, for my part, not to walk "like an antelope" or "like a military man." But there's nothing more difficult than trying to keep pace with someone walking slower than yourself. And I couldn't help feeling a degree of irritation, rather than sympathy, as a result—with all the incomprehension we generally show to the illnesses of others, particularly when they are as yet undiagnosed—worrying quite simply that Foudron's increasingly slow pace was in danger of infecting the project as a whole, compromising its chances of success. On the way, still progressing at his tortoise pace, Foudron pointed out that the yellow school-like building undergoing renovation on the right-hand side of Rue Charles-Michels bore a striking resemblance to Kinshasa's main post office, in a tone implying that I would soon have occasion to corroborate this for myself. The offices of the World Transit Company gave an impression of order and diligence: the business apparently offered the usual legal guarantees, and we were greeted courteously by a team of two—a young man of Congolese origin, or perhaps just Congolese nationality, and a slightly older woman, herself European (the term used most frequently in Africa), whom the young Congolese man invariably addressed as "Maman," in accordance with a custom that does not imply any actual kinship. Maman and the young man quickly grasped the special nature of our project, compared with those they dealt with habitually—they understood, in fact, that the white man was not directly concerned with the commercial side of the operation—but this in no way affected their unruffled serenity, as it had the Château-Rouge contact, nor did it alter the particulars of the information imparted to us. From which particulars it emerged, unfortunately, that World Transit did not do business with the only shipping company with whom I, for my part, had a favorable introduction, thereby complicating my quest for passage along with the car; as well as the fact that the overall cost of dispatching a secondhand vehicle to the Congo was far higher than we had estimated. According to Foudron, even though the car had been given to him for free, the total cost was well in excess of the price of a vehicle in the same condition on the local market. The whole affair was, then, an economic aberration, prompting speculation as to how transfers of this kind could possibly enjoy such obvious success, seeing as the World Transit parking lot was packed with vehicles in various states of repair—some (the most luxurious models) nearly new, and others (the humblest) on the verge of collapse—which, several times a week, were carried off by trucks in batches of eight or ten to the port in Antwerp, where they set sail for Africa. These reflections acted to lower Foudron's morale, and it may have been after that same visit that he first considered giving up on the project, though never telling me as much, and thereby reserving the right, as I suspected later, to place deliberate obstacles in its path—such as arranging for the disappearance of the Opel Corsa—rendering the scheme unachievable *de facto*.

Two days later, I accompanied Foudron to the Paris police prefecture on the Île de la Cité, to collect the temporary residence permit he had been hoping to secure over the past several years. His application for political asylum had been rejected, rightly or wrongly, by the OFPRA (the French Office for the Protection of Refugees and Stateless Persons), and having exhausted every source of help, he had had the good luck—for it was luck indeed, in his case—to have his papers checked by the police, who found them not in order, and to hear from the lips of a low-ranking French police officer that his heart trouble, and the treatment he was receiving, made him eligible for refugee status on the grounds of health, or something like that, valid for six months, but renewable thereafter, and commutable in the long term to a permanent right of residency if, as everything seemed to indicate, his health problems were to prove resistant to treatment. In this way, for the first time, thanks to the cops, Foudron was afforded a tantalizing glimpse of the radiant prospect of a limitless sojourn on French soil, and a long series of medical interventions, admittedly arduous, but efficacious and free of charge. And as bad luck would have it, just a few hours after obtaining the permit in question—a large stamp covering an entire page of his Congolese passport, decorated throughout with watermarks in the form of a lion's head—he collapsed, felled not by a heart attack, as one might have feared, but by a lung infection, the gravity of which his previous medical history could only serve to enhance.

Around this time, the walls of Villejuif were plastered with posters calling for people to vote "No" in the referendum on the European constitution. And such vegetation as was visible consisted almost entirely of tulips, generally red or yellow. In the Infectious Diseases department of the Hôpital Paul-Brousse, Foudron had sole occupancy of a double room fitted with a television. As is generally the case in state-run hospitals and down- or medium-scale hotels, the television was installed high on the wall, on an adjustable support. The set was broadcasting the unfocused, color images of an American cop show, sufficiently low-grade to be scheduled at a time when the only people free to watch it would be old, sick, or otherwise inactive. Although he seemed at first to be asleep, Foudron was following the action with wavering attention: between puffs of steam, his voice slightly distorted by the breathing mask, he mumbled and raised an arm to point out one of the blurred figures on the screen: "He's the one that killed the woman." Next, he invited me to raise the metal window blind and let a little light into the room. Given his uncomfortable position, hooked up to the breathing apparatus and drip, and the painful nature of his lung infection, Foudron showed remarkable placidity, demonstrating his great powers of endurance, and his confidence in the treatment he was receiving. This placidity, as much as his unusual size, and the gallant compliments he dispensed, ensured his enduring popularity with the nurses and orderlies, a popularity that remained undiminished throughout the whole of his lengthy progress through France's public health system. Because between stints in the Hôpital Paul-Brousse, Foudron was transferred to the Hôpital Marie-Lannelongue in the slightly less drab southeastern suburb of Robinson, there to undergo surgery made necessary by the state of his right lung. This complication arose in the first days of May. The life cycle of the local vegetation had now entered a livelier phase: the displays in the flowerbeds at the Hôpital Marie-Lannelongue, like those in other parts of Robinson, offered a variety and profusion far superior to those seen two weeks earlier, in Villejuif. The difference was also, perhaps, attributable to Robinson's higher social standing, and the lower density of its population. As for Foudron, spread-eagled flat on his back once more, his great legs splayed and swaddled in gauze, he was not only hooked up to a drip, but thoroughly piped and drained as well: tubes of every kind fed into his body or out of it, with no perceptible effect on his placidity. Nurses came and went, calling him "Désiré," his real name, and mollycoddling him like a gigantic baby, which, in fact—in his present helpless state—

he did rather resemble. I noted that after several weeks of torment and immobility, his hair had grown gray and kinky on his usually carefully-shaven head, and this had the effect not only of ageing him, but of emphasizing his frail condition. Before his hospitalization, and despite his cardiac problems, Foudron had always seemed to me as solid as a rock. His room at Marie-Lannelongue, more spacious than the first, was lit by a long, tall picture window overlooking the hospital garden and, beyond that, a wooded hill. Above the hill, a great swathe of sky could be seen, dazzlingly bright, although large white clouds were already piling up in the late afternoon, in anticipation of a storm. The window created striking silhouette effects, backlit against the glare outside, and in this way I had my first sight of the two visitors who had preceded me to Foudron's bedside. The first—a tall, thin type with a pale complexion—was introduced as one of his brothers. His comments on Foudron's condition, from his position in front of the window, suggested a high degree of medical knowledge. The second visitor was more reserved, holding back somewhat—at least this was the initial impression he gave, seeing as he said nothing, and seemed equally disinclined to move. His deliberate silence, his regular, impassive features; perhaps, too, his athletic build and stiff, upright carriage—as if he had received high-level fitness training and was keeping himself in top condition—all contributed to an intriguing, novelistic quality, hinting at a backstory with, perhaps, no foundation in reality. Or, who knows, perhaps a little foundation after all. Because Foudron addressed him systematically as "the Major," in a tone of respect colored with camaraderie, and it emerged that they had served together in the FAZ (the Forces Armées Zaïroises) under Mobutu: an episode of Foudron's life—the greater part of it, in fact—which I had never succeeded in mapping out entirely, given that he himself never touched on it, or rarely. The end of this career had been marked by a series of somewhat murky events, as I discovered via the report that Foudron had been called upon to draw up for the OFPRA. His narrative was inevitably colored, however, by the need to satisfy that office's very particular criteria. It emerged that Foudron, having served for twenty years in the FAZ and attained the rank of colonel, had made the eminently reasonable decision not to stand in the way of the troops of the AFDL (the Alliance des Forces Démocratiques pour la Libération du Congo-Zaïre) under Laurent-Désiré Kabila, composed mainly of Rwandans, when, in April 1997, they had overrun the town where he was stationed (it also emerged in the course of the account that Foudron—and doubtless the Major too—was a member of the Luba tribe, from Kasaï province, who had been massacred during Lumumba's brief spell in power: but he himself never mentioned this episode in my presence, nor the role it must have played in his apparently fortuitous decision to enlist with the FAZ some years later). Following this, with Mobutu in flight and Kabila in power, the latter's armed forces took Foudron back, with his former rank, and assigned him to a mission whose special nature only become clear in the course of its execution. While Kabila was running into difficulties in his relations with the international community, and the United Nations showed itself likely to investigate the massacres of Hutu refugees committed by AFDL troops during their conquest of the country—some of which were classifiable as genocide—Foudron and a group of other officers recently returned to the fold were charged by the new powers-that-be to remove all trace of these same massacres. He particularly remembered a point at the intersection of two tracks in the bush, scattered with a large number of skeletons, still bearing "muscles" (his word) in places. Foudron and his men doused the remains with gasoline, reduced them to ashes, and then dispersed these in a stream. He subsequently refused a second, similar mission, as much because of his own scruples as for fear of being liquidated on his return, as had often happened to the witnesses of such atrocities; and it was under these circumstances, after numerous other adventures, that he left Congo-Kinshasa by pirogue to seek refuge in Brazzaville. On the other hand—although I no longer subscribe to this particular thesis—it is also entirely possible that Foudron left his country for France with the sole intention of receiving adequate medical care for his heart problems, after being felled by an initial attack in Kinshasa itself. Whatever the truth of the matter, and if he did indeed find himself alone, a clandestine refugee, in Brazzaville, which was once again in the grip of a furious war between troops loyal to Denis Sassou Nguesso and the "ninja" militias of Bernard Kolelas, it is highly unlikely that he would have succeeded, under such circumstances, in getting out of the country without the help of the Mobutist networks that had reformed in the city after the ousting of their leader. The same networks that have succeeded—rumor has it—in maintaining an armed presence there ever since, driven by a desire for revenge that has lost none of its urgency, ready to cross the river as soon as the occasion presents itself, and seize power once again in Kinshasa. And while I assumed that Foudron, as a good family man, had doubtless steered clear of involvement in such plottings, there was no guarantee that the same could be said of the Major, whose silence, svelte form, and impassive face were entirely compatible with an inclination to underground activities. So that here in the sickroom at the Hôpital Marie-Lannelongue, watching him discreetly, in profile, I wondered (perhaps only in order to complicate matters for myself, or to add a certain unwarranted luster to my own schemes) whether my encounter with the Major, however accidental, would not be a likely source of difficulties later, with the Congolese police, who might be tempted to see me as an agent, a liaison—a miniscule cog, unbeknownst perhaps even to myself, in a conspiracy hatched abroad against the unstable régime of Kabila *fils*. The Major broke his silence only to ask me a few anodyne questions about my previous visits to Zaire (now the Democratic Republic of the Congo), the most recent of which dated back to 1980: a period when Mobutu was at the height of his power and megalomania and the country was sinking quietly into the mire. (That year, I had traveled upriver aboard a barge convoy from Kinshasa to Kisangani, and found myself questioned for the first time, on board the boat, by two cops in plainclothes, very eager to arrest me on some trumped-up charged of espionage. True, the convoy was transporting— among other things—military guns and an escort of possibly North Korean firearms instructors. And on the return journey, on the tarmac at Kisangani Airport, I managed to avoid a charge of "attempted destruction of an Air Zaire aircraft"—a DC-10: my weaponry for the task consisted of one cigarette lighter—only after unburdening myself of a considerable sum of money to a man in rags, pushing a cart, apparently the worse for drink, of whom various signs suggested he was an occasional employee of the national intelligence agency.)

I was in a hotel bedroom in Kiel when Foudron called to inform me of his release from the hospital. Through the window, I could see a number of familiar sights that never fail to put me in a good mood: shipyard gantries, cranes lined up along the dockside, the roof of a railway station, the lines of railroad tracks, and the super-structures of a ferry. Despite the extreme heat—scorching mid-summer temperatures that probably constituted an all-time record on the shores of the Baltic—the room's décor and furnishings, whose paltry inadequacy (rather than actual discomfort) seemed to spring from a long tradition of socialism, combined with the industrial dockside scenery extending in all directions, reminded me of another sojourn in a Baltic city, a city likewise given over to shipbuilding, twenty-five years earlier, but in radically different circumstances, not least of which of was the fact that the earlier episode had taken place in late autumn, when the temperature outside was bitterly cold. The city was Gdansk, in the year during which Poland declared its "state of war," and the scene was a bed-room of the Hotel Hevelius, where I was staying together with a large number of journalists and an even greater number of *zomos*, the national brigade of riot police. Strangely, and even though I must have met Lech Wałęsa just the day before, or perhaps simply tried to meet him, my only distinct memory is of an evening and night at the Hotel Hevelius in the company of a Francophile prostitute, condemned, thanks to my increasingly inebriated state and a strong sense of camaraderie—misplaced as it may seem—to do nothing more (as far as I remember, at least) than make idle chit-chat, in an argot consisting mostly of English scattered with isolated words borrowed from other languages, as well as pantomime. And it was one of these mimes that sprang to mind now, gazing out at the landscape of industrial sites and docks languishing in the heat, through the window of my hotel bedroom in Kiel—a mime with which the amiable Polish prostitute strove to make me understand that she liked not only French journalists but also French hunters: a mime that consisted of bringing her hands up to her ears, fingers outstretched, and which, after many fruitless attempts, and much giggling and guffawing, I finally recognized as her attempt to sig-nify antlers (in particular their sharp endpoints, or tines). Because all the French hunters she had encountered apparently visited the region to shoot deer, and deer with big antlers, if at all possible.

During my stay in Kiel, then, Foudron had finally been dis-charged from the hospital. For my part, during my trip to Germany, in Berlin—a city where poetic license, years after the fall of the Wall, still allows us to rub elbows with double agents—I had met an apparently well-informed character who had it on good authority that the elections scheduled for a few weeks hence in the

Democratic Republic of Congo would be postponed (which did indeed come to pass), and that following this riots would break out all over, because in the resulting confusion, the members of an elite Mobutist troop, the DSP (*Division Spéciale Présidentielle*), armed and supplied by France, would cross the river from Brazzaville and seize power in Kinshasa. (It will be noted that this information went some way toward legitimizing the ostensibly unfounded fears that had beset me after meeting the Major). Officially, the aim of this operation was to rid the country and its government of Rwandan influence, although this had already been severely curtailed during the war with Kabila *père* led by his former allies, Uganda and Rwanda, which the latter had more or less lost after many twists of fortune, at the cost of further foreign interventions and an incalculable number of deaths. My contact maintained that in order to boost the operation's chances of success, containers of weaponry and munitions had recently left the port at Le Havre. Personally, although indifferent to the question of who currently held power in Kinshasa, I feared this plot might ruin my own plans, and worse, that I would find myself caught up in the outbreak of fighting. It later transpired that the man was a sham, and his information didn't hold water, apart from the bit about the postponement of the elections, which was already public knowledge.

Now, with the tiniest of opening moves, driving only from Kremlin-Bicêtre to Vitry, the car began its journey to Kinshasa. This took place on the afternoon of July 2. In the meantime, further difficulties had arisen, such that we had been on the brink of giving up on the entire project. Shortly before mid-June, the Opel had disappeared from its parking space on the curb in Vitry, under such mysterious circumstances—locals thought they had seen it being lifted by a truck fitted with a crane, but it never reappeared in the car impound lot—that for a moment I couldn't help harboring the completely unfounded suspicion that Foudron himself was behind its removal. The reason being that he was back in the hospital, briefly, following another heart attack that had struck him down in the street after emerging from a physiotherapy session for his right lung. And the combined effects of his illnesses, or their treatment, the draining of his financial resources, and the absence of any hope of a return to paid employment—in fact, a whole host of adverse circumstances—had reduced Foudron to a thoroughly depressed state, which depression manifested itself most noticeably in a growing indifference to our scheme. As for the car, I had found us another, the same day, much roomier and more powerful than the Opel Corsa, with brighter paintwork too—blessed, in short, with all the requisite features for conversion to life as a taxi in Kinshasa. The new model was an Audi 80, fitted with a diesel engine. It was twelve years old, with almost 250,000 kilometers on the clock, but it started right away, its bodywork was painted a sparkling metallic gray, and it even included a number of interior fittings and accessories that gave it a certain air of luxury, none of which was to survive the journey. The day we set out to reconnoiter the vehicle, Foudron showed signs of such an advanced state of exhaustion, climbing the hill in Bicêtre, that I was afraid he would die there and then, at my feet. Air escaped from his lungs with difficulty, whistling as it had when he lay on his hospital bed, and his face was covered in sweat as we climbed toward Rue Léo-Lagrange, our destination, so slowly and painfully that on the last (albeit less steep) section of the journey, through a residential neighborhood of small, detached houses, the retired folk peering at us surreptitiously over the hedges of their tiny gardens must have felt like athletes by comparison. Foudron only perked up a little after taking possession of the Audi—albeit strictly symbolically, that day, because after careful consideration, it seemed prudent to secure some sort of insurance in his own name before driving it to his home in Vitry, given that in the Paris region as a whole, blacks at the wheels of secondhand cars run a particularly high risk of being stopped and having their papers checked by the police.

The quest for the aforementioned insurance proved more complicated than anticipated. Foudron thought he remembered a place near the McDonald's at La Fourche: Quick-Assu, offering reasonable rates and coverage for every risk and eventuality, however unusual, and this was where we began our search. But the Quick-Assu employee, in whom long experience of insolvent clients had nurtured tortuous procedural habits, did his best to sell us unlimited insurance, payable by direct debit until such time as he received a document from the prefecture controlling the relevant port of embarkation, testifying that the car had left the country. The fact that Antwerp had no such prefecture (at least not since the fall of the Second Empire) didn't seem to worry him, doubtless because he had spotted an opportunity for Quick-Assu to debit my bank account indefinitely, from here on in.

Later, we found ourselves at Porte de Clignancourt, a neighborhood altogether more suited to marginal (not to say peripheral) activities such as ours. A storm threatened to break, and huge drops of rain were already splattering the pavement. Foudron had resumed his earlier, extremely slow pace, and I couldn't help remonstrating with him—even though his gait was clearly attributable to the state of his health—because he had, at first, assured me that he knew of another insurance provider, even more suspect than the first, on Rue du Simplon, and because now, having gone the full length of the street on both sides, with small shuffling steps, in the advent of the storm, he was wondering aloud whether the office was indeed on this street, or any of the many others intersecting at right angles with Boulevard Ornano, between Porte de Clignancourt and Château-Rouge. After Rue du Simplon, we visited Rue des Poissoniers, with no greater success. In despair, Foudron asked a man selling spare parts for cars, who pointed vaguely along the boulevard to another establishment—not the one we were looking for, but essentially the same. Besides which, time was running out, and soon all the outlets liable to sell us insurance of any sort would be closed. The office pointed out to us by the spare parts salesman was miniscule, and the couple in charge—of indeterminate origin, possibly Bulgarian—exuded an impression of agreeable, almost humanitarian dishonesty: they were, you felt, even more disposed to hoodwink the authorities than to rip off their own clients, although it all came to the same thing in the end, the documents they dispensed being for all intents and purposes devoid of legal status, and conferring only the flimsiest of coverage in consequence. And yet there was genuine solicitude, even respect of a kind, in the way they handled Foudron's driver's license (for example), decorated like his passport with a lion's head—doubtless convinced that the item was a forgery, and inspecting the quality of the workmanship with the admiration of true connoisseurs. We emerged with a piece of green paper delivered on payment of a sum just shy of two hundred euros, a document that would do the job nicely, given that it was needed for nothing more than the journey from Kremlin-Bicêtre to Foudron's home in Vitry, in the first instance, and from there to the World Transit parking lot in Saint-Denis, after which the transporter's own insurance policy would take over.

Not far from the shop was a café with a single table placed outside, by way of a pavement terrace. The storm had not yet broken, and here Foudron and I sat, relaxed and relieved, with a sense of having crossed an important threshold, rendering the whole process irreversible. Our optimism was such that Foudron told me about his arrangements for the car's reception in Matadi, where two members of his family, at least one of whom could drive, would meet me when I got off the boat. Later, in the metro, Foudron remarked on the excessive heat that almost always prevailed on line 4, which he suspected was maintained on purpose by Paris's urban transport authority for the punishment of the line's passengers, many of whom, perhaps the majority—at least on its northern section, at certain times of day—were of African origin. But far from complaining about this discriminatory treatment, it should, he felt, be applied with even greater zeal, taking the temperature, and the resulting levels of discomfort, to still greater heights, if at all possible, because like many immigrants of a certain (relative) seniority, he showed a deep distrust of all those he identified as newcomers, doubtless suspecting them of seeking to usurp his hard-won welfare benefits, or compromising their continuance by sheer weight of numbers.

Our handling of the proceedings (or mine, at least) was marked by a somewhat perverse desire for secrecy (Foudron's own earlier career had afforded ample experience of tracking and trailcovering). Most of our assignations took place in the metro, on station platforms or in connecting corridors. Here, we exchanged documents relating to our joint undertaking, or the administrative procedures (and there were a great many) that Foudron had embarked upon on his own account. Foudron invariably wore black sunglasses, and always carried his papers in an attaché case (also black) that he referred to as his "diplomatic bag." Very rarely, he would also use plastic bags, most often from the Shopi supermarket, an accessory with no established tradition in the genre of spy fiction. For the Audi's first journey, we had arranged to meet at 7:45 P.M. at the exit of the Kremlin-Bicêtre metro station. I arrived a few minutes before Foudron, in time to catch him at the top of the escalator and propel him onto a No. 47 bus that had pulled up at that very moment. We rode the latter to its terminus, then walked a few hundred meters through the same decor of small, detached houses seen on our earlier visit, bathed in the glorious light of the setting sun over the Paris *périphérique*, before jumping into the car—at 8:15 P.M. precisely—and driving off immediately, back down Avenue Charles-Gide, Rue de Verdun, and Avenue Eugène-Thomas to the metro station where we had met thirty-five minutes earlier; Foudron dropped me there, then turned right down Avenue de Fontainebleau and carried on to Vitry. At 8:45 P.M., I had barely emerged from the Tuileries metro station and taken a seat on a bistro terrace to watch the great Ferris wheel turning in the evening air (each cabin—in my fond imaginings at least—carrying a pair of lovers along on its slow gyration), when Foudron called to let me know he had arrived at Vitry without further mishap, having encountered no policemen eager to examine his suspect piece of green paper along the way.

On the day of the car's second move, from Vitry to Saint-Denis—as it happened, on the eve of Bastille Day, July 14—we arranged a meeting at ten A.M. in front of the City Hall in Saint-Ouen. At 10:20 A.M., surrounded by floral tubs shaped like giant mechanical nuts and filled with petunias, I was beginning to worry about Foudron's lateness when he finally appeared at the wheel of the Audi and informed me that it had just experienced its first breakdown. It subsequently transpired that the car's second breakdown (and the burst radiator hose) was a logical consequence of the first. Because the breakdown that had resulted in Foudron's late arrival was due to the fan, which had suddenly stopped working, and would have resulted in the car's prolonged immobilization had it not been for a passerby skilled in the mechanical arts, who had improvised an ingenious, if fragile, linkage that briefly reestablished the flow of electricity to the defective organ in question. Foudron started the ignition and pushed a cassette of Congolese music into the tape deck, in anticipation of the planned outcome of the journey (although not its actual outcome, since the tape deck failed, like every other optional extra, to reach the car's destination intact). In a similar vein, it will be noted that the Audi was beginning its journey on the banks of a modest river, glimpsed through a curtain of plane trees from the World Transit parking lot—a journey that would end, or rather continue, on the banks of another river, far greater altogether.

In fact, the parking lot, and the World Transit company itself, form a small corner of the French department of Seine-Saint-Denis that has become forever the Congo. Here, Congolese customs prevail to such an extent that a single intervention on the part of the female boss, Maman, was all it took to see the Audi loaded as arranged onto the transporter truck standing ready for departure, while the parking lot manager, also Congolese, had intended to prioritize other cars, whose owners had doubtless acquitted themselves of a special levy in his favor. Thanks to Maman's intervention, the Audi was loaded first, once Foudron had made a final inventory of the contents of the trunk (gifts for his family, all of which would eventually suffer the same fate as the tape deck). Many expeditors try to counter the risk of theft en route by soldering shut the trunks or rear hatches of their vehicles, but the soldered joints are easily broken, besides which they also contravene the customs regulations of every country along the way.

Just behind the Audi, on the top deck of the transporter, two Mercedes (one a coupé) were fitted into place, followed by a big, less prestigious Japanese car. The lower deck was reserved for hardier vehicles, generally Volkswagen Combi vans crammed front and back with junk of every kind. Throughout the entire loading process, the parking lot manager traded wisecracks—mostly crude—with the truck driver, a Belgian who had lived in Niger. "I was in road haulage down there too," the Belgian told us, "but it wasn't me doing the driving!" He was a cheerful man, though—apparently unembittered by his demotion. With loading completed, Foudron and I decided to wait for the truck's departure, more out of superstition than any good reason. Between the parking lot and the Seine, on the other side of Avenue Charles-Michels, there extended a sort of no-man's-land where Congolese—or supposedly Congolese—men and women busied themselves in apparent confusion around old engines and other spare parts trickling with oil, probably salvaged from cars so old and wrecked they had been judged unfit for the journey. Behind his black sunglasses, leaning against the parking lot fence, Foudron observed the scene with a condescending air, clearly determined to stand aloof from the inferior level of development suggested by this admittedly archaic bustle. The Belgian driver was less particular, scurrying back and forth between his truck and the no-man's-land, locked in endless confabs with men picking over their engines, doubtless his business associates. At regular intervals throughout, his truck emitted those curious honks of compressed air that make heavy goods vehicles seem such close relatives of the walrus or other marine mammals. The Belgian continued his negotiations, ignoring these calls to order. At 2:15 P.M., he decided to head off at last: the truck rolled out onto the quayside road, and the Audi was lost to sight behind the leafy curtain of plane trees.

During this period I made several trips to Le Havre, mostly to meet with the manager of a shipping company whose vessels regularly served the West African coast. Even before the incident I am about to relate, it had not escaped my notice that the somewhat nebulous nature of many of my schemes, their often rather undefined aims and objectives, or the dubious reputation of the countries and people with whom they sometimes bring me into contact, may have aroused in some people a suspicion that I was involved with the secret service. This is not in fact the case, but the suspicions are undeniably flattering, which is why I have never taken much trouble to dispel them. In any case, denials only tend to confirm your interlocutors' convictions, especially when these are misguided. I have even, on occasion, out of sheer vanity, imagined that I may indeed, at other times, have worked *unawares*, in all innocence, for the secret service. In this way, some apparently aimless or at best futile undertakings found apparent justification or added significance, giving them a renewed luster when, in my own eyes, they had long since lost any hint of sparkle. And so, as I had told myself on my journey up the Congo River in 1980—a journey conceived as a kind of Conradian pilgrimage—I was perhaps serving, blindly, to light the path of flight for Marshall Mobutu, a friend and ally of France at the time, if ever his hold on power were to come under serious threat; and it is a fact that the last years of his reign were indeed spent in large part on the river. (Since that time, I have entertained a kind of vision, imagining how the dictator might have been forced to take refuge with his inner circle aboard his yacht, the *Kamanyola*, sailing upstream to his native province, the only one still showing him some degree of support, and how the stranglehold of the forest, full of little men firing arrows and throwing assegais, slowly closed in upon them, like a reenactment of *Heart of Darkness*, while the presidential entourage tore itself apart with internecine quarrelling, settling the regime's scores in an appalling cacophony before succumbing little by little to attacks of fever, so that by the end, the tyrant, still wearing his leopard-skin toque, shaking his magic cane in vain, robbed of all grandeur, suffered his final agonies alone, spouting fragments of speeches on the deck of the drifting ship, surrounded by rotting corpses and suitcases full of jewelry or banknotes shredded by thousands of little monkeys emerging out of the jungle—this time as in Herzog's *Aguirre, the Wrath of God*—one of whom would make off with the Marshall's toque at the very moment he sighed his dying breath.)

The incident at Le Havre occurred in two parts. On a first trip to the city, with no particular aim in mind, I had met the director of a company that owned a number of warehouses, with whom I spent half an hour or so discussing my activities. A month later, in the same city, I had lunch with the manager of a company whose ships served the African coast (in this case, a man I had known for some time), who trusted me enough to help me with my plan to transport a secondhand vehicle to the Congo, as he had done before in other projects of a similar nature. During the course of our conversation, at the mention of my meeting with the warehouse director, he informed me that the same man, following our interview, had told him that he was convinced I was working, or had worked, for the secret service. And he added that he had found himself completely unable to confirm or disprove this hypothesis. (The fact that I doubtless greeted his revelation with an expression of false modesty rather than disbelief or indignation probably didn't help.) The point being that if I was capable of making such an impression on a first meeting with someone who (I fondly imagined) was himself a former member of the *11ème Choc*, the elite paratroop regiment of the French intelligence services—and that if another person, who had known me for fifteen years, was still undecided on the matter—the inevitable conclusion must be that there is something about me, something in the way I envisage the present or evoke the past as a series of more or less embroidered stories designed to present myself in a favorable light, something, then, that arouses these suspicions to the extent that people invariably find themselves wondering whether they might, indeed, have some basis in fact.

This incident left me, if not shaken, then stirred, and I came away from the lunch, during which my Congolese scheme had made significant progress, nimbed in new glory—that of an Old Intelligence Hand: an honor that was, I assumed, thoroughly undeserved nonetheless.

On the night of July 13 to 14, after the car's departure for Antwerp, I got very drunk: demonstrating a lack of *savoir-vivre*, no doubt, but passing unnoticed in the context of the generalized inebriation that accompanies France's national holiday. I spent the evening in the company of my godson, a quiet young man, but gifted, it seems to me, with great perceptiveness and an astonishing capacity to hold his liquor—a talent that I can't help thinking he may have acquired from me, in part at least. On the evening in question, I began to show signs of confusion, and a certain grandiloquence, while he—having drunk just as much—remained perfectly lucid despite all. My own shortcomings reminded me more and more, as the night wore on, of a scene in the writings of Pierre Mac Orlan, an author for whom I feel a special affection. In this scene, the ambivalent figure of Captain Hartmann—a character I always tried to emulate—drinks in the company of two young people, one a girl and the other her probable pimp, and finds himself suddenly betrayed by his (considerable) advancing years, vanquished by drink for the first time in his life, until he's out cold and has his pockets emptied by the probable pimp. The scene takes place in Hamburg, a city basking at the time (the interwar years) in a certain splendid notoriety. At dawn, he is found lying on the pavement in the red-light district of Sankt Pauli by a member of the *Schutzpolizei*, and accompanied back to his hotel.

My own awakening on the morning of July 14 was less painful, but brought its share of trouble nonetheless. My answering machine bore a message from the agent of the shipping company, informing me that the *Salvation*, my ship for the passage to Africa, had suffered damage and was immobilized. The news came when the car was already in Antwerp, waiting to be loaded at a site from which it would be impossible for me to recover it. So that the immobilization of the *Salvation* might not only bring down the entire project, but cause me a great deal of further hassle besides.

In fact, nothing of the kind occurred. Twenty-four hours after leaving this message, my contact at Le Havre called to offer me a passage on another ship, the *San Rocco*, scheduled to call at Antwerp in the first days of August.

I took advantage of this respite in my preparations for the trip to launch into two cultural undertakings of varying degrees of magnitude: a rereading of Proust, and at the same time, a book by a certain Jerry Allen, entitled *The Sea Years of Joseph Conrad*.

The rereading of Proust, starting with Volume II and leaving to one side the whole of the first book of *Lost Time*, was both the result of chance and a product of necessity. As far as chance, I had initially opened the second volume somewhat absent-mindedly (to all appearances, at least), in order to check the precise nature of the structure—a pier or jetty—upon which the narrator encounters "the little group" in whose midst he first sets eyes on Albertine, to their subsequent mutual misery. The necessity, then—admittedly relative—stemmed from the fact that twenty-five years earlier, as I was to recall that day, leafing through Volume II, I had begun my first reading of *Lost Time* at this exact point, the beginning of *In the Shadow of Young Girls in Flower*, as I was preparing to embark on a journey up the Congo, as far as Kisangani, aboard the push-tug *Colonel Tshatshi*. I had read *The Sea Years of Joseph Conrad* in the same context, but a few weeks earlier, as part of my research into the circumstances of the river voyage that inspired *Heart of Darkness*. The rereading of Proust would take up the whole of my journey in 2005, which itself came to an end just as I finished *The Fugitive*; Jerry Allen's book was skimmed in a matter of hours, but nonetheless afforded interesting insights into the lapses or deficiencies of my own memory. Because the reason why I had taken so much trouble this time around to board ship in Antwerp, rather than Le Havre, for example, or Verdon on the Gironde estuary—regularly visited by ships from the same company—was, for one thing, that the Belgian port is, for commercial reasons unclear to me but probably linked in some small way to customs regulations, far and away the most sought-after embarkation point for the exporters of secondhand vehicles to Africa; and, for another, I had retained, from my earlier readings of *Darkness* and Conrad's biography, the firm conviction that he had left from Antwerp on May 12, 1890, aboard the French ship the *Ville de Maceio* bound for Boma on the lower reaches of the Congo, from where he would set out in turn on the final leg of his voyage to his destination, Matadi. As I soon learned on rereading Jerry Allen's book, however, Conrad had indeed boarded the *Ville de Maceio*, but in Bordeaux, not Antwerp.

Had I chosen to join the *San Rocco* in Verdon, under the administration of the Bordeaux independent port authority, rather than Antwerp, I would not only have spared myself a great many additional difficulties, but also adhered more faithfully to Conrad's itinerary. The choice would have seemed all the more natural given that a few months earlier I had found myself passing through Verdon at the same time as the *Salvation*, the ship I was supposed to have boarded in the first place—a coincidence that I took as a favorable omen. Furthermore, during the visit, I had noticed that Verdon too was a popular embarkation point for large numbers of secondhand vehicles, in addition to other, nobler cargoes, and this despite its somewhat out-of-the-way location. And finally, as I discovered around the same time, reading a packet of letters passed on to me, curiously, by a cousin (curiously, because the letters had been in her possession for many years, and she knew nothing of my planned trip and its preparations), it was also in Bordeaux that my father, forty-three years after Joseph Conrad, had boarded a ship bound for Africa, for the very first time.

All of the letters passed on to me by my cousin were written by my father to his parents, and were, as a result, marked by a reserve bordering on insincerity. In them, he takes great pains to present himself as the model son—which he was not always, it seems, to judge from scattered references to his debts, and a brief spell in a military prison toward the end of his studies at the naval medical academy in Bordeaux. In the first letter, which must date from October 1933, under the heading "aboard the *Foucauld*, Wednesday evening," my father writes that the ship he has just boarded was immediately shrouded in thick fog, forcing it to drop anchor for several hours in midriver near Bassens. With my habitual tendency to spot coincidences wherever I go, I noted that shortly before receiving these letters, which were never intended for my eyes, I had visited Bassens quite by chance, for the first time in my life, on a day when the river Garonne, viewed from the heights of the town, had disappeared beneath a thick cloak of mist, which only cleared in late morning. This was, no doubt, virtually an everyday occurrence in the region. What was less so, however, was that during this first visit of mine, on a walk beside the temporary moorings along the riverfront at La Pallice, I had come across several large pieces of the *Foucauld* lying in the open air—watched over by a security guard and dog—recently salvaged from the shallow water where they had lain rusting since the beginning of the war, when the ship had been severely damaged during a bombing raid, after which it had been towed and scuttled some distance from the foreshore.

Some of my father's letters, collected in the bundle, described his first sojourn in Africa, mostly in the area of present-day Mali; others refer to his second trip, spent almost entirely in the area between the Ubangi and Sangha rivers, both tributaries of the Congo. And in particular, it seems, along a river bisecting the angle formed by these two, known by the curious French name of Likouala-aux-Herbes. His correspondence is interrupted after a letter dated May 11, 1940, written in Likouala, where he makes no reference at all to the war in Europe and its recent developments, about which he clearly knew nothing at all. My cousin also included a handful of later letters in her package, but these are written in the hand of one of my uncles, apparently also in Africa, in a region that subsequently remained under the control of the Vichy regime, from where he tried unsuccessfully to get news of my father. It is amusing to see how, once the colony of the Congo had rallied to the opposing Free French cause, he denounces those he refers to unequivocally as "dissidents" (the Resistance) and, initially at least, asserts his firm belief that my father could not have joined such a mad undertaking. Then, over the course of several letters, still with no news, his conviction wavers, and he begins to wonder whether "Jean"—this was my father's name before me—might not have allowed himself to get drawn into dissidence nonetheless, not out of patriotism (this possibility doesn't seem to have crossed my uncle's mind), or a simple refusal to accept defeat, but egged on by his own "vivid imagination" and the "reckless impetuosity of the amateur reporter." And in this he was not, perhaps, entirely mistaken.

On Tuesday August 2, in midafternoon, an enormously violent storm broke over Antwerp and the surrounding region. On the Noorderlaan, beyond the curve described by the road parallel with Zesde Havendok, where visibility could have been no more than two hundred meters, an incessant stream of trucks continued to pass in both directions—some pulling huge sea containers— throwing up great sheaves of water. Other containers could be seen on the left-hand side of the road, piled five or six high, and it was here, through an opening in the stacks, that my driver first caught sight of the Wilmarsdonk bell tower. At the start of the ride, in front of the Hotel Docklands on Italiëlei, I had given the bell tower as my destination. Even then, he only saw it because he knew to look for it there. And we lost sight of it again before the taxi found another road likely to bring us closer to it. The road in question, Treurenberg, was set at an acute angle to the Noorderlaan, or more accurately describing what is commonly known as a hairpin turn: to turn onto it, the taxi had to pull over to the right-hand lane of the Noorderlaan for some time, blocking the line of heavy trucks advancing on that side of the road under sheets of rain, then hold up the dense traffic of trucks bearing down at high speed in the opposite direction. The weather conditions gave the entire operation the air of a naval battle on the high seas, with the taxi as a torpedo boat cutting across a convoy of battleships advancing single-file through the raging storm, immediately under the stern of one of their number. The rain began to abate just as we turned onto Treurenberg, and it had stopped completely by the time we pulled up at the entrance to a dead end between two huge walls of containers at the far end of which a not insurmountable wire fence was the only thing separating us from the bell tower. The tower stood alone, its base overrun by wasteland scrub, in the middle of a zone now used for freight storage, but which was once the site of the village of Wilmarsdonk. Doubtless it had been spared for religious or superstitious reasons (always assuming these are not one and the same). Built mostly of brick, it was not of any great architectural interest, despite its relative age—it had probably been built rather later, in fact, than the rest of the village of Wilmarsdonk, which had not been granted a similar reprieve. The tower bore witness to a sense of guilt that later communicated itself to all who came across it in its abandoned state—it had been spared, but apparently unmaintained ever since. It was hard to see it as any kind of consecrating presence for the site it overlooked; the 1/17,500 scale map of Antwerp records it simply as "Wilmarsdonk Distribution Zone 380." I had been told that the

Audi would probably be awaiting embarkation somewhere around here, parked in an open-air enclosure with other vehicles, both new and used, bound for export to Africa. But it was, I thought, probably unwise to try climbing the wire fence to see for myself, thereby risking arrest and being mistaken for one of the very car thieves I feared would try to strip the vehicle I was supposed to be transporting. In any case, my pilgrimage to the Wilmarsdonk bell tower, shortly after arriving in Antwerp, had been undertaken for other reasons, with little real hope of locating the Audi.

That morning, a girlfriend had dropped me in Paris near the Gare du Nord for my assignation with Foudron, who had insisted on giving me his final instructions in person. He was dressed for the occasion in an elegant two-tone shirt with short sleeves. And no black sunglasses. His new "diplomatic bag"—the first had fallen to pieces—was fitted with a theoretically impregnable security lock, giving it the appearance of a portable safe. From this he withdrew a sturdy brown paper envelope containing letters for his wife and his remaining dependent children—two boys and two girls—followed by a few small items destined for one or other of the above, and photographs that would help me identify them when we met in Kinshasa. Clearly, he judged this visual reconnaissance aid to be insufficient, and insisted that we also call them from a telephone booth outside the station. And so for the first time, on the forecourt of the Gare du Nord, I heard the voices of Clémentine (his wife), and his two daughters. I noticed that Foudron called his wife *ma chérie* and spoke to his daughters with great tenderness. Having accompanied him several times on shopping trips for his family, and knowing how proud he was of his children's grades, I had never doubted that Foudron was a good father and a good husband. And it was in this capacity that he had conceived the plan; the revenues from the taxi—from the Audi-turned-taxi—were intended to supply the needs of his immediate family, not his extended family (his instructions had been very clear on this point), and in particular to pay for his children to attend private schools, state education having long since withered and died in the Congo, if indeed it ever really existed. The minutes that followed were marked by a certain solemnity, appropriate to the circumstances, all the more so when Foudron, wishing me *bon voyage*, observed that I would be seeing his country again "before him," implying that for his part, there was every chance he would never see it again.

The agent for the shipping company in Antwerp went by the name of Van der Meersch, a man whose appearance and conversation radiated that pervasive aura of pessimism with regard to human nature so often observed in his fellow Belgians. Throughout the journey from the Hotel Docklands to Churchill Dock, where the *San Rocco* was moored, following the same route taken the previous day by the taxi, Van der Meersch held forth in great detail about the many risks incurred by vehicles travelling "naked" (without the protection of a shipping crate) between Europe and Africa, and which were not, according to him, limited solely to the potential for thefts on the part of longshoremen and other dock workers in the African ports. Even on board ship, Van der Meersch was eager to stress, it paid to keep a close eye on crew members with access to the lower decks where the vehicles were parked; some of them wouldn't hesitate to lift the odd spare part to supplement their meager pay—increasingly so, since the ship owners, registering their vessels under exotic flags, had delegated responsibility for recruiting and managing their crews to companies unburdened by an excess of scruples. And my Belgian contact had failed to mention the predations to which the vehicles were prone even before embarking, in the holding areas around the port (perhaps because he was unaware of these), although the extent of such trespasses was quite apparent from the quantity of shattered Securit glass littering the area where I presumed the Audi had been kept, just off the Churchill Dock at the foot of the Wilmarsdonk bell tower. Now that I had found it again, the bell tower followed me everywhere. I could see it from the porthole of my cabin, rising above the huge storage sheds and piles of containers, after being introduced to the *San Rocco*'s commanding officer by Van der Meersch, who had accompanied me up the access ramp. The captain, a small, mustachioed Pole, remained impeccably polite while at the same time giving every impression of having found out just there and then that I would be spending several weeks on board the ship he would be commanding for the next few months—because like the rest of the crew, he was employed not by the ship's owner, but by an agency registered on the Isle of Man—and seemed completely disinterested in the matter, handing me over to the First Mate, another diminutive Pole, but a great deal younger, who showed me to my temporary quarters; the other, more spacious cabin set aside for me was occupied that night by the outgoing captain (the ship was taking advantage of its stop in Antwerp to change crews). The First Mate was marginally more communicative than the Captain, and seemed better informed about my plans. But although he had certainly heard about the Audi, he could offer no tangible proof that it had been loaded aboard the *San Rocco*—my own investigations had established only that it was no longer in the glass-strewn parking lot—though he showed himself very willing to help, promising me that once the ship had set sail, and as soon as conditions allowed, he would take me on a visit to the lower decks, so we could reassure ourselves. I would be sailing out of the port of Antwerp, then, with no certainty whatever as to the car's fate, leaving me with no option but to disembark at the next port of call if it was found missing. If this scenario proved true, and the car had been loaded onto another ship following the same route, it would be all but impossible for me to catch up with it and prevent it from disappearing without trace during its transit through the Congolese port of Pointe-Noire. At every stage of the process, the most difficult thing was always to ensure that the car and I advanced in tandem, and this difficulty only increased as we drew nearer to our destination, when the need to keep a close eye on the vehicle was matched only by the equally pressing need not to be identified as its owner, or indeed connected with it in any way at all, thereby hopefully attracting no attention whatever to the bizarre circumstance of a white man traveling by cargo ship with a used car, from either the inevitably ill-intentioned authorities, or anyone else liable to interpose themselves in search of gain. The cabin in which I was installed for the night had been occupied previously by a painter (in the industrial sense) named Dmytro Tokar. His efforts, or those of his predecessors—for Dmytro Tokar was doubtless one of a long line of temporary workers recruited by the agency registered on the Isle of Man—to make things a little more home-like, to connect the cabin to dry land in some way, had achieved some measure of success, insofar as it was now suffused with the stuffy, rather rancid atmosphere of a bedroom in a hotel for migrant workers. To be fair, the permanent fixtures—or at least those fixtures not the responsibility of the cabin's successive occupants—contributed greatly to this effect, especially the photographs decorating the walls (baskets of fruit and flowers, or colorful rustic landscapes), apparently dating from the era when the ship was first constructed. On the other hand, Tokar and his fellow mariners had doubtless contributed over time to the collection of pin-up photos, the lace cloths partly covering the coffee table, a Chinese calendar for the year 2001, and the extraordinarily large, zoomorphic ashtray—a plaster rabbit lying on its stomach in a familiar Bugs Bunny pose, leaning on its elbows and holding its chin in hands, ears cocked, or rather one ear cocked and the other folded forward halfway down, bearing on its back a tiny saucer for the receipt of cigarette butts.

The *San Rocco* was moored starboard side to port, and the cabin, on deck 7, faced that way, its porthole offering a view that embraced not only the installations on Churchill Dock, dominated by the solitary bell tower of Wilmarsdonk, but also a whole section of the city of Antwerp, shrunk in the distance to a frieze of slender or squat silhouettes, discernible as church towers, belfries, high-rise blocks or offices. Throughout the loading procedure—which is to say until the middle of the following afternoon—the ship's hull shuddered at irregular intervals in response to the heavy or gentler

thuds of the containers installed on deck, or the momentary tor-
sions communicated to its structure by the heavy goods vehicles
climbing the access ramp or moving around inside the hold. And
every moving thing—cranes and vehicles alike—was accompanied
by the incessant noise of alarms.

When the *San Rocco* set sail on the afternoon of August 4, cutting itself off from dry land with the lifting of its gangplank, detaching itself gradually with the dropping of its hawsers, it was one hundred and fifteen years to the day since Joseph Conrad himself had set sail in Kinshasa aboard the steamer *Le Roi des Belges* for the journey upriver that was to inspire *Heart of Darkness*.

In those bygone days, between Matadi and the shores of Stanley Pool, a certain Prosper Harou took thirty-six days (with thirty-one native porters and at least one other white man) to complete the route that the Audi would cover (despite the burst radiator hose) in slightly less than twenty-four hours: Harou whom Jerry Allen identifies as "a corpulent Belgian official of the Free State who, after a leave spent in Europe, was returning to his station . . ." For his part, W. G. Sebald in *The Rings of Saturn*—with his usual disinclination to quote sources—reiterates the figure of thirty-one porters, but, while spelling Harou's name in the same way as Allen, describes him as an "overweight Frenchman," adding that he "invariably fainted whenever they were miles from the nearest shade." Why, assuming he took his information at least in part from Jerry Allen's book, did Sebald make this unpleasant, ridiculous character a Frenchman (and my compatriot) when everything, logic included, points to his having been a Belgian? At first, I attributed this substitution of nationality to anti-French sentiment, conscious or otherwise, given that Sebald chose Britain as his adopted homeland, and doubtless took on some of his hosts' prejudices. Because it may indeed have been an unintentional slip, albeit the only example of its kind in Sebald's work, at least to my knowledge. But a few pages later on, in the same book, Sebald unleashes a series of violent anti-Belgian diatribes, demolishing my earlier hypothesis. "And indeed, to this day," he writes, for example, "one sees in Belgium a distinctive ugliness, dating from the time when the Congo colony was exploited without restraint and manifested in the [. . .] strikingly stunted growth of the population." "I well recall," Sebald continues, "that on my first visit to Brussels [. . .] I encountered more hunchbacks and lunatics than normally in a whole year." Clearly, the substitution of nationality does not reflect a desire to appease the Belgians. Perhaps Sebald was inspired by another biography of Conrad, in which Harou is identified as French. Or perhaps, simply, he got his notes muddled. (Jerry Allen's book goes on to point out that the passengers on board the *Roi des Belges* included a commercial traveler by the name of Rollin, with two *L*s: this form of the name is very common in Belgium.)

After passing through the Berendrecht Lock, connecting the Kanaldock to the Escaut River, I was installed in my new quarters on deck 9, just below the bridge, a cabin once occupied by the ship's radio operator, until technological progress and the demands of trade sounded the profession's death knell. Moving from the painter's cabin to that of a radio operator took me several rungs up the social ladder, albeit within the same overall cultural context, its references unchanged. Hence, the dayroom adjoining the cabin—which was consequently reduced to the size of a roomy burial chamber (a comparison reinforced by the complete absence of windows, unlike the dayroom, which was lit by three portholes)—the dayroom, then, was decorated with the same landscape views as Tokar's cabin, with the exception of a few minor details, albeit more carefully executed, and larger. One picture showed a woodland scene in autumn, traversed by a path scattered with yellow and red leaves; the other showed another leafy landscape with a foaming river cascading through the middle. Far from evoking thoughts of dry land—as might, for example, a reproduction of Rosa Bonheur's painting *Ploughing in the Nivernais*—both landscapes suggested nothing at all, or perhaps a kind of bucolic purgatory where mankind was fated to expiate his sins against Nature in a state of eternal ennui, so that it was impossible, even after attentive examination, to identify a specific country or region of the world, the most likely answer being that the paintings depicted nowhere at all, but were wholly synthetic, the result of pure invention. The view afforded by two of the three portholes (whose effect the decorator had probably intended to counter with his idealized landscapes) was blocked by a white-painted structure housing the ship's main elevator, to either side of which the sea could be seen passing beneath the starboard wing bridge, but the third porthole took in the entire rear section of the ship, dominated by its funnel and the gantry against which the raised access ramp rested like a titanic, decommissioned guillotine.

Despite the small sign posted in the passage leading to the dining room (along with other threatening notices issued by the agency registered on the Isle of Man), reminding the crew that "English [in red] is the only official language on board this ship," everyone spoke chiefly Polish or Russian (or Ukrainian). Most often, however, silence (or discretion) reigned, at least in the public areas, especially those where the various ranks of the ship's hierarchy were liable to fraternize. It seemed likely that the men were more inclined to talk among themselves out of the presence of the officers, for example during chess matches or their occasional games of backgammon, during their off-duty hours, around the picnic tables installed either side of an atrium on deck 6 (the only dining room, of vast proportions, being located on deck 5). The officers' and crew's messes were also on deck 6, on either side of the atrium, but neither was used except for watching video cassettes or playing video games, by those men—the majority—whose cabins weren't fitted with the necessary equipment. The boat had been built by a Norwegian shipping company, and as a result its facilities were for the most part comfortable, spacious, even somewhat oversized in places, while others had become so due to the reduction in crew size, and the remaining crew's increasingly rare group activities. Hence the officers' mess, generally deserted and dark, was arranged like a small concert hall with seats covered in red velvet and portholes masked by curtains of the same color. At the far end of the room, the lines of seats were interrupted by a monumental table, apparently the work of an artisan in one of the African ports served by the ship, its varnished top supported by two lions carved from the same wood. Above the table hung a portrait of a surly-looking woman, who may or may not have been the Queen of Norway. The whole setup looked ripe for the celebration of a Black Mass or some sadomasochistic rite, and totally unsuited to more everyday uses. In the dining room—with the exception of my first evening, when I dined alone due to the presence of the supernumerary captain—I shared the Captain's table with the Chief Engineer and the First Mate, all three officers Polish. Personally, I would have preferred the table allotted to the three lieutenants who took turns at the permanent watch on the bridge, two of whom were Ukrainian and all of whom were younger and more relaxed than their superiors, but I was not given the choice. For the first few days I kept silent unless spoken to, so as not to appear indiscreet (of all the different preconceptions surrounding life at sea, the one pertaining to the sailors' distaste for talkative types is among the most accurate), and allowing the Captain and the Chief Engineer to talk, albeit succinctly, in Polish. The First Mate spoke only rarely. Later, given the age of the Captain and the Chief Engineer—old enough to have witnessed or taken part in the events marking the decline and fall of the socialist regime in Poland—it seemed to me that it would be possible, even proper, to allude to this period, taking as my pretext the fact that the ship had been built in 1980, the heyday of the *Solidarność* trade union, at the Paris Commune shipyard in Gdynia. I had also noticed that the ship was fitted with a Sulzer engine manufactured under license by Cegielski, a company in Poznań that distinguished itself in 1956 with a strike during which some fifty workers were killed by the militia. In 1982, I had occasion to visit Poznań and passed by the entrance to the Cegielski plant, above which there still hung the slogan, "The Party unites the vital forces of the Polish Socialist Nation."

But neither the Captain nor the Chief Engineer seemed at all interested in this episode of their history, although the latter did bear a certain picturesque resemblance to Lech Wałęsa. Admittedly, by venturing into this territory I had infringed another rule of maritime etiquette, which forbids the discussion of politics on board ship. Not only did the Captain not take up the conversational line I had thrown him, but in the course of the discussion, and subsequently, he expressed such virulent, extreme anti-American and Slavophile sentiments, and such a degree of skepticism on the subject of democracy—especially the "free" press, whose content, he observed, was almost as far removed from reality and ideologically skewed as that of the official press under communism—that I found myself wondering if he wasn't one of those Poles in whom the *ancien regime* inspired a certain nostalgia, the more so because as an officer of the merchant navy he had probably enjoyed a relatively privileged status in those bygone years, perhaps every bit as enviable as that now afforded him by the agency registered on the Isle of Man. Nonetheless, the Captain was proud to be the owner of a small house, all his own, near Cracow, and a big dog he was always asking his wife about whenever the ship drew near enough to land to permit the use of cell phones. His love of big dogs, and his loathing of environmentalists, whom he regarded as "terrorists" every bit as dangerous as the members of Al Qaeda, if not more so, marked him out as a man of order. The Chief Engineer showed a similar cast of mind, although more out of the sarcastic amusement inspired in him by "intellectual types," an attitude for which I paid dearly when my limited appreciation of the ship's supply of terrible Hollywood movies on video led him to suspect that I belonged to that category of snobs or idiots (in his view) who swore only by films made in "Kazakhstan, Georgia, or China."

The sides of the garbage trucks parked at the back of the quay, alongside other decommissioned vehicles, some of which would be loaded onto the *San Rocco* during its time in port, bore a slogan in French, repeated on each: "People of Marseilles, the time has come to respect your city!" Had this injunction, in its day, succeeded in dissuading the Marseillais from their old habits, convincing them never again to dump their trash wherever they saw fit? We may well wonder—just as we may wonder how the slogan would be understood by the inhabitants of whichever African metropolis was to be granted the privilege of receiving the secondhand trucks. Most of the other vehicles were buses of various national origins, lined up along the open holding area, empty, their engines running, hydraulic doors open to minimize the effects of the heat, their sheer number and decrepit state—together with, strangely, the confusion or apparent irrationality of all these engines ticking over in the absence of any sign of a driver, or indeed activity of any kind—suggesting preparations for some mass deportation or exodus. Or perhaps this impression was due to the fact that slipped in among them was a small green pickup truck, loaded with the carcass of a car, not only registered in Bosnia-Herzegovina but still advertising the name of the company to which it had belonged there—Autopravoznik, in Gradačac—and that of its former proprietor, one Dedić Ferhad.

From the wing bridge, vast expanses of marsh and salt pasture were also visible, drained by canals, and stands of pine or deciduous trees—the *landes* that extend along France's southwest Atlantic coast, in the middle of which stood a water tower, and beyond that, the village of Verdon. And everything languished in an oppressive early afternoon heat whose effects were felt most strongly after descending the access ramp, crossing the open holding area, and advancing between the white wall of the storage shed and the railway tracks toward the automatic gate and its adjoining kiosk, beyond which lay an expanse of open countryside, or scrub.

Eric and Delphine were waiting for me in their car on the road leading to Verdon. I knew that meeting up with friends at a port of call might complicate things for me: by reinforcing not only a sense of alienation with regard to the surroundings one has briefly left, but also a sense of familiarity with a different context altogether, such encounters run the risk of completely undermining a cargo passenger's early efforts at acclimatization. Among the favorite habits of people on dry land, which one has to learn to do without at sea—aside from seeing friends from time to time, rather than the same set of Ukrainian merchant seamen every hour of the day—there is that of shopping in the local supermarket (in this case, the French chain Champion). I could probably have done without a renewed acquaintance with this particular activity, but I had a pressing need for liquid soap (preferably my favorite no-scrub brand, "ideal for hand washing or prewash stain removal on all textiles"), and after searching in vain along the shelves of an open shop in the village of Verdon, we found ourselves in the parking lot of a supermarket near Soulac-sur-Mer. And the spectacle of the parking lot, and then even more that of the supermarket itself, the crowds hurrying inside, thronging its aisles, waiting in line at the check-out counters, in a frenzy of familiar activity tinged, it seemed, with a hint of insouciance or devil-may-care, which was discernible too in the prevalence of seaside attire—because they were, for the most part, people on holiday—all this threw me into a kind of giddy disorientation, as if having one foot aboard the *San Rocco* and the other in the midst of the holidaying families of Soulac-sur-Mer robbed either option of any sense of reality. On leaving the supermarket, we decided to reinforce the holiday atmosphere and headed for the Pointe de Grave, where a long beach borders the ocean, surprisingly deserted but for a handful of anglers. The beach's emptiness, even in the summer season, is due to violent currents and rough surf, so that I didn't swim, but merely took a dip in the water, keeping at least one foot firmly on the ground (the supermarket experience had taught me something, after all), while Eric, fearless in the face of danger, managed to swim for a short distance along the shallows, and Delphine lay on the sand. After this, we left the ocean for the estuary. On the beach at Chambrette, as calm, friendly, and populated as the other was wild, fierce, and deserted, the holiday atmosphere peaked with the presence of makeshift beach cafés, their terraces shaded by roofs of straw or palm fronds, where we were served by pretty girls with bare midriffs. I was in need of a drink by now, but worried that if I started, I wouldn't be able to stop, or at least not before displaying symptoms that were unlikely to fool the Ukrainians (or Poles) I would be rejoining later and who—quite unjustly, as I was later to discover—I had decided rather vaguely were all ex-convicts, due to their close-shaven heads, which gave them the look of prison inmates, but which were probably insisted upon by the agency registered on the Isle of Man. It also occurred to me that drinking, in the short space of time left to me ashore, would only exacerbate the super-market syndrome, my momentary sense of being nowhere at all. Just before the time appointed for my return to the ship, Eric and Delphine dropped me at the dock. I walked back along the length of the storage shed wall, crossed the open holding area, where the garbage trucks still stood with their exhortation to the people of Marseilles—clearly, the *San Rocco* would not be taking them to their destination after all—but which was now empty of buses, and walked up the ramp on which two Ukrainians, covered in dust and sweat, dressed in orange overalls (the same, I thought to myself, as those worn by the detainees at Guantánamo), were busy fixing patches of rust. My appearance clearly marked me as a man who had spent the entire day engaged in leisure pursuits, but still I was relieved that my swimsuit, at least, was invisible, con-cealed inside the Champion supermarket bag with my soap and two bottles of Bordeaux, presents from Eric and now the object of a growing quandary as to how I should set about distributing them, or not, between the Captain's table and that of the three lieutenants. I now regretted not having bought two more, but in reality I would have had to bring aboard an entire case to share with the crew as a whole, thereby risking the disapproval of the higher ranks, not least because the rules laid down by the agency registered on the Isle of Man stipulated that the *San Rocco* was, in principle, a "dry ship," aboard which the consumption of alcohol was strictly forbidden.

I had, perhaps, a tendency to exaggerate the complexities of ship-board protocol, the more so because as the ship advanced toward Africa, I too was making progress with my rereading of *Lost Time*. Hence, the day I reached the episode in which the narrator is introduced to the Duchess of Guermantes was also the day I received notice of an invitation to the "ten o'clock coffee," a daily event at sea involving the Captain, the Chief Engineer, and the First Mate, in the Captain's office. The invitation arrived the day after we had called at Verdon. On the previous night, the ship had put to sea several hours later than planned. Through my cabin window, I had watched the light fade and the stars appear above the mud flats and salt pastures around the port terminal, while on the quayside a chorus of alarms rang out, accompanying the sequenced movements of the gantry crane and power lift trucks, loading containers. This activity continued until around midnight, followed by a brief moment of relative quiet that served to magnify the vibrations imparted to every part of the ship's structure by the engine as soon as it was restarted (vibrations that communicated themselves, irritatingly, to certain items of cabin furniture, almost always the same ones—the glass-fronted toilet cabinet or the cupboard doors—which had to be listened out for, pinpointed, and neutralized by the judicious insertion of bits of cardboard), after which the *San Rocco* had put to sea. At around one o'clock in the morning, his task complete, the Verdon pilot had been winched up by helicopter, an event I recall in precise detail, because I was standing in the dayroom adjoining my cabin at the time, and because the helicopter was positioned directly overhead throughout the maneuver. Hence, the following day—or rather, that same day, nine hours later—when I attended the Captain's coffee get-together for the first time, after staying a while on the bridge, innocently (as I thought) consulting the ship's log, I committed an opening *faux pas* by pointing out what I believed was an inaccuracy: the pilot's departure, for reasons that were unclear to me but doubtless the result of nothing more than simple oversight, had been recorded at three o'clock in the morning, two hours late. When I made my observation, the Captain—far from congratulating me on my interest in the running of the ship, or providing me with an explanation for the mistake, if such it was— simply stared at me with one eyebrow raised and asked if I was "in the habit of looking through ship's logs," as if I had been caught reading his private correspondence. After this the conversation, in English, took a friendlier turn, although my presence, and with it the obligation to resort to a foreign language, doubtless robbed it of much of its usual spontaneity. The Chief Engineer in particular said nothing, perhaps because he wanted me to feel I was an unwelcome intruder, but more likely out of shyness, and because he was by nature a man of few words. The Captain launched once more into a series of diatribes against the environmentalists of this world, as if, having allowed myself to become tainted by their doctrines, he was doing me the favor of setting me straight—particularly as I had just shown an interest (misplaced or excessive in his view) in a handful of land birds, including a gray heron and a warbler, who had outstayed their visit after our stopover at Verdon, and of whom it seemed quite reasonable to wonder whether they would ever get another opportunity to return to shore, failing which, fluttering endlessly around the ship or seeking precarious shelter among the containers on deck, they were threatened sooner or later with death from thirst or hunger). The Captain's sentiments were echoed by the First Mate, who contributed a personal anecdote highlighting some little-known and unpleasant characteristics of whales, about which environmentalists (and the media whose pockets they lined) maintained a notable silence. One day, said the First Mate, he was suspended alongside ship in the mid-Atlantic, almost level with the tops of the waves, in order to patch up a spot of paintwork or carry out repairs of some sort (a highly unlikely scenario that cast doubt over his account as a whole), when a school of whales had surrounded him, close enough for him to smell the odor of the liquid spurting up through their breathing-holes, which liquid—and this was his point—was foully pestilential. Because, added the First Mate, the stench undermined the "romantic" image of these animals, as generally propounded to the public at large, predisposing people in their favor.

At 10:45 A.M., the captain, while in no way departing from his habitual politeness, began to show discreet signs of impatience, making it clear that the get-together was drawing to a close. At this point, however, he forgot to specify whether my invitation should be considered permanent or extraordinary, so that the next day, fearful of upsetting him by not showing up if invited, or by showing up if not invited, I was forced to lurk in the passage near his office, keeping a discreet eye out for the small table at which coffee was served, until the number of cups set out by the Ukrainian steward Pan Dimitri (three or four) would enable me to answer my own question with a considerably reduced margin of error.

On the morning of Thursday, August 11, passing Cape Finisterre with the silhouette of sheer cliffs discernible in the mist—a last chance for the heron and warbler, neither of whom, it seemed, was in a fit state to seize it—the First Mate, unusually with a few minutes of free time at his disposal, offered to take me down into the hold and check whether the Audi was indeed, as he thought, somewhere on level 3B. The hold of a roll-on-roll-off ship may seem like a vast tunnel at first glance, but in reality, and on closer inspection, it is much more like a burrow dug by some ingenious, provident animal, consisting of an entire network of movable galleries arranged on different levels, which can be connected or temporarily cut off from each other as necessary. So that with the hold fully loaded, the only approach to the walkway on level 3B—a subdivision of level 3, as its name implies—was to thread between the containers loaded on deck (down the middle of which, along the central axis of the boat, there ran a kind of deep chasm), take a right turn into a gap about two-thirds of the way along, and climb down a vertical ladder to level 3C, from where a ramp led to level 3B. Here, the vehicles were so closely packed that it was almost impossible to get around other than by walking on their roofs. Their arrangement also made it impossible to read the registration plates. After a few tentative identifications, I finally recognized the Audi, noting that from this angle, in the half-light, it had appeared to have suffered no significant damage beyond a few dents.

The reconnaissance of the Audi was followed a few hours later by a blackout on the part of the warbler. I was standing on the bridge at the time, the only part of the ship where I was almost certain not to get in the way, apart from my cabin (which I avoided for extended periods, for fear of making too much headway with my rereading of *Lost Time* and arriving in the Congo bereft of further reading matter), and where it was easier to engage in unfettered and increasingly friendly conversation, there being only one person on duty as a rule (very exceptionally two), and that person invariably being one of the lieutenants (either the Pole or one of the two Ukrainians), all three of whom I liked. The youngest of the two Ukrainians, Yevgeni, was from Odessa. His face was pockmarked (like his country's president, Viktor Yushchenko, albeit nowhere near as badly) but unlike Yushchenko, he professed complete indifference, even a certain hostility, to the Orange Revolution, an attitude attributable to the Russophile prejudice of his country's proletariat. Despite this, we shared a liking for the French-Canadian singer Mylène Farmer—as I discovered one day when he showed me a video clip of her on his portable computer—as well as, to differing extents, Napoleon, the swashbuckling French pirate hero Surcouf, and *The Three Musketeers* (in fact, he was an ardent fan all around of what little he knew of French history and popular songs). His compatriot Olex had slightly more seniority in their rank, and such a high degree of pessimism that he expected little good to come of his country's putative admission to the European Union. Upon hearing about the Audi for the first time, he assured me with even greater peremptoriness than Van der Meersch that it stood no chance whatsoever of arriving safe and sound at its destination. Olex was a circumspect character who could seem withdrawn at first. He brought the same care and attention to the dismantling of a French press as he might to the defusing of a powerful weapon. And he refused to sweeten his tea with anything but honey produced in the traditional, time-honored way by one of his neighbors in the Ukraine. Of the three lieutenants, Arkadius the Pole, to all appearances barely more than a boy, was the only one likely to find favor with an average cohort of Western intellectuals, despite his fervent Catholicism, which was tempered with a superficial acceptance of the common ground of modernity, making him pleasant and easy to talk to, with none of the post-Soviet prickliness or awkwardness of the other two. And it was on one of Arkadius's two daily watches, between the hours of four and eight P.M., that the warbler's accident took place. The lieutenant had been showing me his latest holiday photographs on his portable computer, as well as some pictures of Pope John Paul II's hometown, when the incident occurred, putting me in a difficult position yet again: I was far more concerned with the warbler's plight than I was with Arkadius's photograph collection, but afraid that I might hurt his feelings by appearing uninterested in the latter, even for a moment, in order to concentrate more fully on the former. At this point, the captain appeared on the bridge, compounding my discomfort and embarrassment: unsure as to whether or not the lieutenant was guilty of professional misconduct by consulting his holiday photographs on his personal computer during his watch, I was equally unsure as to whether I should stop looking at said photographs (thereby avoiding bringing them to the Captain's attention, but at the same time betraying my own fickleness and hypocrisy to Arkadius) or continue examining them with redoubled interest, out of solidarity with Arkadius, thereby giving the Captain to understand that his lieutenant had offered to show me the pictures out of politeness, at my own request. On the other hand, I was tempted take advantage of the Captain's arrival and leave the two of them to sort it out themselves while I investigated something I had spotted a few seconds before, namely the warbler's reappearance after an absence of twenty-four hours, fluttering over the portside wing bridge, following which it had, almost immediately, flown straight into a pane of glass.

It now lay flat on its back with its claws curled, as in death, on the wooden deck. The illusion persisted for a couple of seconds, giving me time to bend over the tiny body, with its olive-green back and yellow belly. Then, before I was able to take hold of it, the warbler revived. Immediately—and stupidly—instead of eating the bread I had crumbled for it into a saucer bearing the shipping company's crest, it flung itself headlong into an exhausting flight around the ship's superstructures. After dinner, on Yevgeni's watch, the warbler took refuge inside the bridge itself, perching momentarily on the various navigational instruments, then on my wrist, where it stayed for a few seconds, cocking its head to look at me with its beady eye, elegantly outlined in yellow, but not long enough for me to take advantage of our newfound intimacy and conduct it over to the saucer of crumbs. In truth, the warbler's choice of my wrist as a perch was no mark of favor, but simply a sign of the bird's disorientated state—apparently, it had mistaken me for a tree. And despite my efforts to hold on to it, it soon flew off outside and went back to fluttering in all directions before landing on the radar mast, where I could see it through binoculars, wobbling its head and screwing and unscrewing its neck like a man afflicted by uncontrollable tics. We never found the body, a circumstance that left us unable to mourn or "embark upon our grieving process" (as some television news presenter might have commented, after announcing the "death, earlier today, of a warbler"). But it would seem that the tiny bird died in the hours that followed, of thirst and exhaustion.

And three days later, when the *San Rocco* encountered large flocks of terns and skuas off the coast of the Western Sahara, I observed them with real pleasure—some fishing, others trying to relieve the fishers of their catch—delighted that here were birds perfectly capable of coping on their own, needing no care or attention whatsoever.

Among the missions undertaken by the Supercargo, and recounted by him years later aboard the *San Rocco*, one involved trawling the entire Monrovia agglomeration to recover shipping containers that had been stolen from the port area and put to a variety of unwonted uses, as retail outlets (at best) or (at worst) for the storage and mass execution of prisoners, as witnessed by one crate in particular, its sides riddled with bullet holes and its interior encrusted with dried blood, until the time came when the horrors he witnessed crossed a particular threshold, and he requested passage home. Another mission of this type had taken him to Luanda, the capital of Angola, a country in the grip of a conflict whose death toll was still, at the time, unacceptably high. On our current, peacetime, voyage, transporting the Audi successfully over the equator, the Supercargo joined the *San Rocco* during its stopover at Abidjan, charged with smoothing out all manner of difficulties ahead with regard to the ship's payload and

dealing with the relevant port authorities. Of these, he was a con-
noisseur. The Supercargo brought with him just eleven crew boys
from Côte d'Ivoire, six of whom were engaged in maintenance
and warehousing tasks for the whole of their time aboard, while
the remaining five took care of security, chiefly consisting of the
repelling and expulsion of stowaways. Both groups disembarked
two weeks later at San Pedro, the *San Rocco*'s last port of call in
Africa before its home voyage, back to Europe.

On Saturday, August 20, in the late afternoon, the ship presented
itself at the entrance to the Vridi Canal, connecting the ocean with
the sheltered lagoon of the port of Abidjan. The sun had dipped below the horizon some minutes earlier when the pilot came aboard.
After which the *San Rocco* stood down, as in a doorway, to make
way for a roll-on-roll-off ship operated by Linea Messina, painted
bright orange. When the *San Rocco* made its way into the canal,
the noise of the engine (slow ahead) was muffled, and we heard the
sound of waves breaking on the beach extending out from the left
bank, visible from the portside wing bridge but cloaked in a layer
of mist that seemed to thicken before my eyes, casting deeper and
deeper doubt on the nature of the left bank itself: was it open scrub,
as suggested by the waves breaking noisily on the deserted shoreline
and the ragged outlines of bushes just visible behind, or was it an
orderly plantation, as suggested by the tops of the coconut palms,
neatly aligned, emerging from the mist in greater and greater numbers as the ship progressed along the Vridi Canal? While the right
bank unquestionably belonged to the city and industry, the left
bank afforded a glimpse of a village at the junction of the canal and
the lagoon, its sandy thoroughfares lined with shacks and, in the
middle of a dusty open space, a community house where the entire

population, it seemed, had gathered at nightfall to listen, religiously, to the voice of an angry man issuing from a loud-speaker—a voice whose energetic pronouncements it was impossible to identify as either sacred or profane (and, in the latter case, whether they might refer to the current political situation in Côte d'Ivoire), any more than it was possible to tell, from the portside wing bridge, whether the orator was addressing the crowd live from inside the community house, or via a broadcast.

Later, the Supercargo told me the village was populated by fishermen from Ghana, and that they had suffered reprisals in the past—the village may even have been set fire to at some point—when their national team defeated that of Côte d'Ivoire in a football match.

As soon as the *San Rocco* had completed its docking maneuvers, and lowered its ramp to the quay, it was boarded by dozens by dockworkers, preceded up the ramp by the Supercargo and the eleven crew boys. Of these, the security team—soon to be clad in orange overalls—made an initial check of the dockworkers' identity papers before admitting them to the ship's hold, where they scurried with not a moment to lose as soon as the checks were completed to take charge of the pallets of salt sacks loaded in Dakar, from which there seeped a briny ooze that had long since made the deck uncomfortably slippery and crusty (sounds of metal chains and snap hooks clattering on the metal floor, alarm signals: the hold was emptied of a portion of its cargo, and filled by a compensatory cloud of exhaust fumes pouring from the forklifts and other vehicles).

Inevitably, the arrival of the Supercargo necessitated a certain fine-tuning of the etiquette governing life aboard the *San Rocco*. It also, to an infinitesimally small degree, altered my own status. In view of his rank in the ship's hierarchy, it was entirely correct for the Supercargo to take his meals at the Captain's table: but given that the latter afforded only four place settings, this meant banishing the First Mate, who, unable for some reason to eat with the three lieutenants, although closer to them in age, now took his meals alone at the table nearest the Captain's, which had stood empty until the arrival of the Supercargo. (It was here that I had dined on my first evening aboard, in Antwerp, ceding to the supernumerary captain the place that I was subsequently to occupy at the definitive Captain's table). The First Mate was, perhaps, secretly relieved by this. Because, although he seldom spoke at the Captain's table, he was nonetheless obliged to take an interest in the latter's sporadic conversation with the other two diners. For my part, inevitably, the presence of a French speaker at the Captain's table—and better still, a Breton from Saint-Malo—made me far more talkative, especially given that the Supercargo, as demonstrated by his stories of Monrovia or Luanda, boasted a deep knowledge of the region coupled with a very particular perspective, rooted in personal experience, on shipping, maritime trade, and contemporary African history. While in no way appearing to take offense, the Captain nonetheless commented to me, with a hint of irony, that "the time for silence is past." Another problem presented itself when the Supercargo unhesitatingly and categorically declined to take part in the ten o'clock coffees. Such offhandedness, or such unaffected simplicity of manners, only heightened my own discomfiture and made it still more intolerable: the Supercargo's example showed just how easy it was to extract oneself from these seemingly pressing obligations, with no apparent repercussions. Perhaps the Captain had been offended by the Supercargo's refusal, nonetheless? And what would happen if, following the Supercargo's example, I took the decision to stop attending the ten o'clock gathering? In other words, had I not taken such pains to attend, would the Supercargo have been able to get out of it quite so easily? Clearly, no such calculations entered into the Supercargo's decision—his scant concern for matters of protocol was such that every morning, after settling sundry difficulties relative to our forthcoming ports of call by telephone, he would install himself on a deck chair, in full sunshine and in full view of the bridge, with no concern for the jealousy or resentment this might provoke in the other officers, not to mention the crew, who were generally so ashamed to appear inadequately occupied that none of them had dared to suggest filling the onboard swimming pool, since the *San Rocco*'s entry into tropical waters.

On Tuesday, August 23, at three minutes past eight in the morning, at the very beginning of Yevgeni's watch, while the low clouds reflected in the bluish walls of the empty swimming pool, and the Supercargo's deck chair stood equally empty nearby, the ship crossed the equator at a speed of three and a half knots. One hour after sunrise, the outside temperature was 23°C. It rose steadily as the day wore on. Arkadius's watch had just ended, and he was still on the bridge when Yevgeni arrived to take over, armed with the bottle of Coke and the Snickers bar that constituted his usual breakfast, together with a handful of L&M cigarettes. Yevgeni had crossed the "Line" forty times, he said, and felt no more excitement in this regard than anyone else on board the *San Rocco*, while I remembered more conventional expressions of enthusiasm—shouts and horseplay, ritual dousings in seawater, etc.—under the same circumstances aboard the *Alain LD*, twenty-five years earlier, as it prepared to enter the mouth of the Amazon, welcoming aboard the Macapá pilot (already, early in the day, showing signs of mild inebriation). Later, a series of innocuous-seeming events took place aboard the *San Rocco*. First the ship came to a halt, a fact I became aware of—in my dayroom with its three portholes, where I had just crossed the threshold of La Raspelière a second time—thanks to the sudden silence of the engine, and the resulting lull in shipboard vibrations. Then, almost as suddenly, the ship began to list heavily to port, so that my reading of Proust (and my reception at La Raspelière) continued in circumstances more evocative of Conrad, in particular the episode in *Lord Jim* when the hero errs through indecision and sets his life on the fateful course that will shape his entire future. To discover the reason for this change in the ship's situation, still stationary, and listing now to about ten degrees, I went up to the bridge, where Olex, the taciturn Ukrainian, was on watch. The Captain was nowhere to be seen, and Olex was impassively smoking a cigarette, suggesting that nothing dramatic was going on, unless both lieutenant and Captain had taken leave of their senses and decided to scuttle the ship on the high seas. I saw that one of the crew boys, clad in his orange overalls, was also on the bridge, whereas ordinarily neither he nor any of his counterparts had cause to set foot there, and may even have been forbidden—*de facto* at least—from doing so. Olex's silence, and that of crew boy—who, I noticed, brought his hand up to his left eye at regular intervals, the latter swollen and red as if from a blow—together with the rolling motion of the ship, considerably amplified by its motionless state, and the myriad cracking and grinding noises that resulted, all suggested, if not a shipwreck, then at least a mutiny. Although it was hard to imagine how the eleven crew boys could have taken over the ship unaided—quite apart from the fact that, until then, they had all shown boundless devotion to the Supercargo, whom they invariably addressed as "Super"—and harder still to imagine an alliance, even a tactical one, between the eleven crew boys and all or part of the regular Ukrainian crew. And all this time the ship, still listing ten degrees to port, continued to roll and creak, while Olex carried on smoking and the crew boy persisted in massaging his hurt eye, while out on the horizon there appeared the silhouette of an island, probably volcanic, capped with two tall peaks and perfectly compatible with the mutiny hypothesis. This hypothesis collapsed only after Olex invited me to have a cup of tea, and act as interpreter between himself—in his role as the ship's acting medical officer—and the crew boy, who had gotten a sliver of metal in his left eye while repairing a patch of rust. In the infirmary, I explained to the crew boy in detail how he should apply a coating of ophthalmic ointment procured by Olex to his lower eyelid, and gave him several packets of Kleenex from my personal reserve, in exchange for which he showed me a touching gratitude—until the end of the voyage—that revealed the extent of his innocence and generosity of spirit.

The ship's immobility, it turned out, was due to nothing more than an engine problem that was repaired in a matter of hours, during which the Captain had taken the opportunity to wash away the coating of brine and encrusted salt on the deck, and to evacuate the water by ballasting the ship far enough for it to run off the raked surface.

On the evening following the mutiny—with the *San Rocco* on its way once more, vibrating all over to the regular rhythm of the Suzer engine manufactured under license by Cegielski—a full moon rose surrounded by clouds, while the remains of the day lingered on the horizon, making the dark waters gleam like some Romantic landscape painting evocative of sad things, the death of a maiden heroine perhaps, her body rolling now beneath the ocean waves. And with Nature herself embracing such bad taste, such indulgence in the pathetic fallacy, the resulting scene was so persuasive that, contemplating the shining black expanse, the

broad swell rising and falling in the moonlight (an image of infin-
ity, perhaps, rather than nothingness?), it occurred to me, briefly,
that if I were to throw myself overboard from the portside wing
bridge, I would meet a seemingly horrific end—torn apart by the
ship's propeller or devoured by sharks—but nobler, nonetheless,
and with a greater promise of posthumous glory, than the "slow
and painful" death announced daily to French smokers by their
cigarette packs.

What matters most about Denis Sassou Nguesso is his excellent reputation in the oil and gasoline industry. That he succeeded in claiming (or reclaiming) power by force, at a cost of many tens of thousands of lives and the partial destruction of his country's capital city, Brazzaville, and that he held on to power, for example, by massacring his former opponents on their return to that capital after promising to spare their lives, or that before making himself immeasurably rich he had long proclaimed his devotion to Marxist-Leninist doctrine, probably in complete ignorance of its true nature—all this counts for nothing, or very little. Because many African, and non-African, heads of state have done as much, and the world's most bountiful reserves of oil and gas are generally to be found in the earth beneath their feet.

The morning after my arrival in Pointe-Noire, I was told that Denis Sassou Nguesso was celebrating his daughter's marriage—in fact, the girl was one of his nieces. Convoys of upscale Peugeots plied the city streets, dark and gleaming, topped in some cases by revolving lights, sweeping all before them and testifying to their manufacturer's affectionate benevolence, like that of the oil industry, toward the reformed Marxist-Leninist president. Pointe-Noire is, notwithstanding all this, a pleasant holiday resort, with a continuing (or renewed) French presence of such strength that with the exception of one or two minor details, the visitor might think he had returned to the controversial era before independence (or, in the particular case of the decor of the La Citronelle tearoom in Pointe-Noire, as it looks today, transported more than forty years back in time to the Perugina patisserie and ice-cream parlor in Dakar, Senegal).

My last moments on board ship were marked by acute anxiety at the prospect of finding myself back on dry land, and forced once more to confront the difficulties involved in transporting the Audi. On my last evening in the dayroom with its three portholes, I had made good progress with Volume 4 of *Lost Time* (*Sodom and Gomorrah*), before becoming absorbed in the contemplation of the few familiar, graceless objects from which I would soon be taking my leave, together with the habits I now associated with them: the wire coat hanger and peg on which I hung my T-shirts after washing them with the liquid soap bought in Soulac-sur-Mer, where they would swing gently back and forth with the rolling movement of the ship, an image that inevitably suggested, whether I wanted it to or not, a hanged man.

Several hours before arriving at Pointe-Noire, at nightfall, the constellated lights of drilling platforms and oil rigs began dotting the horizon, on structures shaped mostly like watering cans or oilcans, their elongated spouts spurting flares of differing heights. And the reflected glare of the flames lit the ceiling of low cloud with a shifting brilliance across its shifting expanse, as they billowed out with greater or lesser ferocity, making the sky not uniformly red, but mottled like a mass of ashes, still incandescent in places, and cooling in others. The *San Rocco* passed the port jetty, entirely dark due to a power outage; by the light of her own lamps, with the propeller drawing up a pale, ominous cloud mass from the black waters of the basin, the ship seemed to feel her way to her allotted bay on a section of quayside that looked as if it had once been rammed—lined with logs, giving it the rustic appearance of a landing stage at the edge of a forest, rather than a dock in an industrial port.

At around eight o'clock the following morning, the Audi disembarked, driven by a dockworker from deck 3B to the parking lot of the storage company with whom I had arranged to leave it, in sight of their offices, in order to dissuade scavengers tempted to harvest any of its parts. When it rolled down the ramp and set off along the dockside, I noticed that two of its signal lights were broken, and its bodywork was dented or scratched in a number of places—details that had escaped me when I had visited the car at sea, in the semidarkness of deck 3B, and even during the stopovers in Dakar and Abidjan where, constantly afraid of having it stolen, I had spent as long as possible at the car's side. While one of the dockworkers maneuvered it through the hold, in an atmosphere once again saturated with engine noise and exhaust fumes, I tried to make conversation with one of his colleagues, who showed a certain anti-imperialist hostility at first—Sassou Nguesso's volte-face did not, it seemed, extend to every echelon of society—before softening and confiding in great secrecy that his name was Jacques. Still, Jacques found my plan to tell the story of a car in a book somewhat absurd, and he accused me of contributing to the region's underdevelopment by importing a used vehicle. I might at least have made the effort, he felt, to buy a new one. Admittedly, some of the models disembarking from the hold of the *San Rocco* were in a sorry state, to the extent that a few refused to start, while others moved forward only reluctantly, on flat tires. The dockworkers showed little concern for the cars, driving them to the parking lots like drag racers, after which the vehicles sat for varying lengths of time before being released at last by customs, in some cases, or else, in others, being re-exported. In daylight, it appeared that the quay where the *San Rocco* was moored had recently been used to store raw timber, which explained how, trampled by the tire or caterpillar tracks of heavy trucks, and thickly carpeted with impacted strips of bark roughly the color of powdered chocolate, it had acquired such a rustic, sylvan appearance. A few logs still lay scattered around the open area, and there was also a long articulated truck belonging to a circus based in southern Brittany. The circus promised entertainments that would cause their spectators to "die laughing," and there was something pathetic about the thought, on this open dock area in the Congo, of year after year of badly paid, dejected circus artists (as I imagined them) presenting the same clown act day in, day out, to their Breton audiences, for the most part completely impassive, with the possible exception of the children.

One of the crew boys, in charge of security at the bottom of the ramp, explained how much easier his task had become now that the logs had mostly disappeared. Before, he said, the would-be stowaways often hid among them in large numbers, in the almost always fruitless hope of getting aboard the ship. Such an undertaking had even less chance of success given the presence, on the edge of the open holding area, of a small building housing a handful of soldiers—almost certainly corruptible, admittedly—one of whom, upon catching sight of me, strode over, not in order to arrest me on some trumped-up charge of espionage, as I had feared, but to ask in sign language for two cigarettes which I hurriedly provided. Beyond the military building the holding area, covered with low vegetation dotted with purple flowers, was unsuitable for commercial activity of any kind, and still farther off it gave way to a beach with rolling waves and white sand, crisscrossed by the delicate claw marks of terns who flew off at my approach and other, deeper, tracks betraying the presence of one or more stray dogs.

My sojourn in Pointe-Noire lasted for nearly a week while I waited for the cargo ship *Banana Pride*, which was to take the car and me as far as Matadi, on a twenty-four hour voyage beginning at sea and ending on the river. I took advantage of these unexpected few days' holiday—aboard the *San Rocco*, despite my own indolence, perhaps because everyone else around me was constantly busy, I didn't feel as if I was on holiday—to make headway in my re-reading of *In Search of Lost Time*, and to immerse myself in Conrad's horrifying description, in *Heart of Darkness*, of Matadi and the slavery still endured at the time by thousands of men, who were first rounded up, then forced to work building the railway connecting Leopoldville with the lower reaches of the Congo. (With regard to this construction project, W. G. Sebald, in *The Rings of Saturn*, gives the figure of several hundred thousand deaths per year—in other words hundreds, up to thousands of deaths per day, a crime that he says was "nowhere mentioned in the annual reports" of the Société Anonyme Belge pour le Commerce du Haut-Congo, but which first "came to public attention in 1903 through Roger Casement, then British Consul at Boma," and a future martyr of Irish independence.) I had also collected a substantial, but sadly uneven, body of documentation about the conflict that broke out in 1998 between Laurent-Désiré Kabila (together with his new Angolan, Zimbabwean, and Namibian allies) and his former (Ugandan and Rwandan) allies. Although this conflict began in the eastern province of Kivu—if we discount a prior attempted coup in Kinshasa—its repercussions had extended as far west as the region around Matadi, following a rebel operation of such daring that it came close to toppling the regime, before eventually leading to its own destruction. The rebellion broke out on August 2, 1998; the next day, while the attempted coup d'état was held in check in Kinshasa, and fighting spread throughout the east of the country, members of the Rwandan military seized three civilian aircraft on the tarmac at Goma Airport, in Kivu province. On August 4, loaded with several hundred men, the airplanes flew over the entire expanse of the Democratic Republic of Congo, from east to west, landing near the Atlantic coast on the military airbase at Kitona, which was immediately seized and overrun without a shot being fired. (Rumor has it that in this instance, the Rwandan military made use of their dollars rather than their munitions.) From this base, consolidated in the days that followed by Rwandan and Ugandan military reinforcements also flown in by air, the uprising threatened Kinshasa, a few hundred kilometers upstream, and secured control of the Democratic Republic of Congo's small window onto the Atlantic. Shortly after this, the seizure of the Inga Dam upstream from Matadi deprived Kinshasa of electricity. At which stage the Kabila regime's days were, it seemed, numbered.

As for Matadi, the date of its fall to the rebels is given by some sources as August 15, and August 20 by others. The town seems to have surrendered without much of a struggle, the Congolese troops (mostly survivors of the FAZ—the Forces Armées Zaïroises: i.e., Mobutu's army) showing little appetite for combat. But from August 23, things began to look worse for the rebels. On that day, after some hesitation, Angola—a country sharing a vast border with the territory in question—decided to respond to the situation with military intervention, fearing that its own armed opposition forces might take advantage of a rebel victory in the Congo. In just a few days, the Angolan army, supported by Zimbabwean forces, reversed the situation completely, crushing the rebels in Kitona, then chasing them successively out of all the positions they held in the region. Matadi was taken back in the last days of August. My sources lacked precise details on the subject, but it seems that the city was retaken without significant fighting around its perimeter. Nothing comparable, at any rate, to events at Kitona, where it is said, that the Angolans "took no prisoners." In other regions of the Democratic Republic of Congo, the war continued for several more years, until the signing of a fragile accord safeguarding the interests of most of those responsible for the fighting, the terms of which still govern life in the country today.

The hotel in which I was installed by the shipping company—known as the Guest House—was on Avenue Barthélémy-Boganza, not far from the intersection with Avenue du Général-de-Gaulle.

A nightclub had just opened opposite the hotel, already with some claim to the title of chicest joint in Pointe-Noire, in which capacity it generally opened its doors no earlier than eleven o'clock at night. Every evening during my stay, I promised myself a visit to the nightclub, and every evening I was tucked into bed, most often buried in *Lost Time*, by the time it opened for the night. Several times, appalled by my own excessive indolence, or cowardice, I made a show of getting up again and putting on my shoes, then gave up on the idea, terrified at the prospect of even stepping through the door of the establishment on my own, and perfectly sober, there to be assailed by dozens of girls, too rushed and overwhelmed to choose the one with whom I might conceivably want to spend the evening. And if I opted for a wholesale refusal of their services, I was sure to earn myself an appalling reputation, guaranteed to reach the ears of staff at the hotel, and beyond. Not that the girls were devoid of charm, of course—they were not, on the whole, as I found when I came across them during the day in the corridors of the hotel, or on its forecourt. Failing anything else, one or other of them would sometimes ask me for 2,000 CFA francs to buy "a drink of Coke." They were insistent, but almost always pleasant about it.

My nearest neighbor in the hotel was a military man, probably one of Sassou's retinue, as I discovered one morning when a member of staff began knocking on his door, then beating it with redoubled force, calling out "Colonel! Colonel!" in an increasingly loud and, it seemed to me, angst-ridden voice. No doubt the Colonel was just dead drunk after abusing the liquid hospitality offered to Sassou's entourage after the President's niece's wedding. But for a few moments, while the hotel worker hammered on the door and called out in anguish, I was afraid he would be found dead, and, worse still, in the arms of a prostitute. I imagined the consequences of his death under such circumstances for the girl and, to a lesser extent, the hotel's other clients. (And yet, I told myself, Foudron himself had been a colonel; Foudron who had just left me a message, asking how things were going, and what he should do with regard to the next stage in our plan.) As for the frequentation of nightclubs, my life in Ponte-Noire was tantamount to that of a retired, low- or middle-ranking civil servant. Every morning, I would set out in search of French newspapers in a bookshop where I was certain to find none whatsoever, or at best a copy dating from some weeks back, robbed of any import or value, even if it did summarize events that had taken place during my time at sea, and thus unknown to me. Failing that, I would buy the Congolese papers, all of which were so bombastic and confused that I was unable to tell whether they supported the authorities' point of view or criticized it; one explanation for this obfuscation—in all fairness to the Congolese journalists—being the need to give the censors the slip, behind an effective smokescreen.

At lunchtime, I dined on Breton crêpes at La Citronelle—the tearoom whose decor and atmosphere were so curiously reminiscent of Dakar in the 1960s. Sometimes I shared my meal with the driver placed at my disposal by the company, an astoundingly pious man, almost always recovering from an entire night spent praying with the pastors of some "Church of the Awakening," or preparing for the next.

In the afternoons, I occasionally took an excursion with my driver to the border with the Cabinda enclave, or the tennis (or golf) club, where I would leaf absently through the guest book, full of photographs of meals attended by whites and a much smaller number of blacks of comparable social rank and status.

In the evenings, I would walk in the darkness, back up Avenue Barthélémy-Boganza to the intersection with Avenue Général-de-Gaulle, declining a good half-dozen propositions for sex with often highly attractive girls along the way, before settling down to dinner on the terrace of Le Kactus, a restaurant frequented mostly by expatriates. From my table, I could see the illuminated sign of the Total gas station on the other side of the intersection, just opposite that of a branch of Crédit Lyonnais with its ATM, and a little further away, on Avenue Général-de-Gaulle, another sign indicating the site of the Air France office. For a Frenchman, there was little danger of culture shock on the terrace of Le Kactus. Still less on the menu, from which I invariably chose a pizza (a particular variety called the "Ninja"—appropriately enough, this was also the name of one of the militia groups that had clashed a few years earlier in the country's succession of civil wars) and a bottle of Ngok beer, with a label showing a green crocodile on a yellow background. Often, a group of giggling girls—there for the expats—would dine at the next table, sparking regret, in some cases, for my earlier decision to steer clear of them. Seated below the terrace wall, members of staff talked among themselves, sometimes in French, sometimes in a language that was probably Lingala, with the result that whenever the conversation began to get interesting, it also became completely incomprehensible, at least to me.

"Lovesickness can kill," said one, "I can see very clearly that you're suffering, you don't know it yourself, but me, I can see it. Your father suffered," he went on, "and you, you want to suffer like your father. Personally, I will never have a woman in my house." But when the stricken lover started developing his counterargument, and perhaps defended the women who make people suffer—or the men who like to suffer at the hands of such women—it was in Lingala.

When Foudron called, late in the morning, I was preparing to leave the Guest House and make my daily rounds: first the bookshop with its newspapers dating back several weeks, then La Citronelle, with its appealing, old-fashioned Dakarian atmosphere, and the Breton crêpe (a *complète* with ham, cheese, and eggs) taken with or without the born-again driver whose nights were spent in fervent prayer. Foudron wanted to know the name of the ship I would be boarding with the Audi, and the date on which it would set sail (this last detail had already changed several times since our last conversation). The date and time were now fixed, give or take a few hours; consequently, the same margin of uncertainty was imputable to our time of arrival in Matadi. What was now less certain however—and for unforeseen reasons—was my own likelihood of accompanying the Audi on this last section of its voyage. Because a new difficulty had arisen, two days earlier, when the local maritime prefect had given notice that I would not be allowed to travel as a passenger aboard a cargo ship, or at least—as far as he was concerned—that I would be unable to disembark from such a ship at Matadi, and enter by this means into Congolese territory.

For my part, I assumed that the prefect had produced this last-minute difficulty solely in order to exact an additional fee: but he could also plead, and fairly, the threat weighing down upon him and all other officials involved in the impending visit, any day now, from the U.S. Coast Guard, on a mission to ensure that the port of Matadi had taken the necessary measures in the fight against international terrorism. And it was only too clear, in this context, that my disembarkation from the *Banana Pride* at Matadi would reveal a flaw of the first order in local procedures. Not only was Foudron irritated by these delays—and myself even more so (if I was forbidden to accompany the car to Matadi, it would never reach its intended owners, and all the obstacles overcome earlier would have been for nothing)—but he could hardly hear me, so that I had to shout into the telephone on the forecourt of the Guest House, spelling out the name of the *Banana Pride*— "Bravo, Alpha, November, Alpha, November . . ." and suffering an obstinate lapse of memory, for some reason, when it came to the phonetic alphabet word (Papa) associated with the letter *P*. Over lunch at La Citronelle with my driver, of whom I was unable to tell whether or not he really did live in fear of hell, nor indeed what his personal idea hell might be, I noticed a Filipino man (hence almost inevitably a sailor) at the next table, eating alone and sporting a cap with the badge of a shipping company by the name of Marlowe, whose Conradian connotations I took to be a good omen (although, as I was to discover later, it was just another offshore agency).

During the course of the day, the company's representative in Pointe-Noire provided me with hourly updates on the progress and outcome of his negotiations with the maritime prefect at Matadi. Sometimes it was yes, and I hurried to the Guest House to pack my bags because the *Banana Pride* was leaving that evening, but sometimes no, and I was overcome with despair, because my planned alternatives—such as taking the Congo-Océan railway from Brazzaville to Kinshasa, and some other mode of transport from there to Matadi—left me no hope of arriving in time to oversee the unloading of the car, running the risk that it would, quite simply, disappear. It was also possible that the recipient whose name figured on the docket—a relative of Foudron—would be charged with failure to collect his package within the stipulated time, and forced to pay a fine far beyond his means. In this scenario, not only would Foudron and I lose face, but his family, far from benefiting from the car, would be faced with insurmountable difficulties because of it. I too, at times, resigned myself to this outcome, experiencing that curious satisfaction, often accompanied by bursts of hilarity, provoked by the sense of having failed utterly, and just short of reaching one's desired goal (to pull myself together, I thought of Walter Houston's laughter at the end of *The Treasure of the Sierra Madre*, when he discovers that all the gold dust has blown away on the wind).

At around five P.M., I was informed that the misunderstanding with the prefect was in the process of being resolved—a wad of notes had doubtless been mobilized to this end, somewhere along the line—and I was free to embark, although some doubt remained as to what sort of welcome I would receive in Matadi. A little later, presenting myself for boarding at the *Banana Pride*, I noticed first, with pleasure, that the captain was the same Filipino I had seen lunching alone at La Citronelle, and, second, with some concern, that the Audi had already been winched aboard— the *Banana Pride* was a traditional cargo ship, not a roll-on-roll-off like the *San Rocco*—and secured with other vehicles on top of the containers loaded on deck: it would, then, be traveling in the open air, exposed to the elements (it was already coated in a thick layer of yellow dust, turning to mud in the humid evening air), and would have to be winched off again in Matadi, multiplying the risk of bumps and scratches, and the general deterioration of its condition.

The entire crew of the *Banana Pride* was Filipino, with the exception of the First Mate, a Ukrainian, clad in the usual orange overalls and with his hair tied back in a ponytail, currently occupied in directing the loading operations. He allowed me to pull one of the Audi's doors open, as a result of which I saw that certain accessories, such as the tape deck, had already been stolen, while other extraneous objects had been introduced, including a hubcap that didn't match and some old strips of rubber.

During my short time aboard, my most frequent contact was with the First Mate. But it was only in Matadi, waiting for the authorities to decide my fate, that I had the opportunity of an extended conversation with him, during which I learned, for example, that he had spent two years in the Soviet army, serving in Afghanistan and specializing in the maintenance of rocket launchers. Like many former citizens of the Soviet Union, the First Mate wasn't shy about expressing his scorn for all the delays and procrastination inherent in the democratic process, and his preference for the expeditious solutions of the great tyrants, notably Stalin, but also Hitler, both of whom he nonetheless classed as "crazy people," a judgment tinged with a marked hint of admiration. He sometimes interrupted his stories—including a magnificent account of his hunting expeditions in the Izmail marshes, tracking giant boar: trips that often extended over an entire week, punctuated by manly drinking sessions, prompting inevitable comparisons to the opening sequence of *The Deer Hunter*—to strike the mess wall with his fist, declaring "I love this ship!" or "God bless this ship!" as if trying to convince himself of his (in reality, perhaps rather inconstant) devotion to the vessel after six months on board. In truth, and despite the eccentric or downright abhorrent notions he sometimes professed, the First Mate was a sympathetic character, constantly animated by an exhausting level of nervous energy—he often complained of having lost the ability to sleep—as is often observed in men with long experience of combat, particularly in the context of a war that's been lost in advance, and generally waged against civilian populations.

I woke in the middle of the night, with the ship already off the coast of Pointe-Noire, surrounded by drilling platforms. Opening the bedside table drawer in my cabin (once again, I was occupying the former radio operator's quarters, but aboard a ship far larger and more spacious than the *San Rocco*), I found two paperbacks belonging to a certain E. R. Dioquino who, in addition to his name, had scribbled the date September 4, 2001 in one of the books (*The Golden Gate*, by Alistair MacLean), and May 25, 2003 in the other (*Alan Marshall's Australia*). The drawer also contained a copy of the *Manila Bulletin* dated July 16, 2005, a bottle-opener with a Beck's logo, and the business card of a certain Najib Labrini, "Naval Architect, Surveyor, ISM/MarSec Auditor," apparently living in Casablanca and affiliated with the Moroccan office of Germanischer Lloyd.

At daybreak, the ship rose on an extended, sidelong swell in the brown water, marbled with trails of gasoline and dotted with islands of accumulated floating vegetation. And from out of this stew, there nonetheless emerged a whale—a short distance from the ship—puffing out a jet of its stinking liquid (as claimed by the First Mate of the *San Rocco*) before diving once again, its tail fin held vertically for a few seconds. The First Mate was on watch, still sporting his ponytail and calling down blessings upon the *Banana Pride*, before being relieved by the Captain as the ship approached Banana, where it would take on board its first pilot, to be relieved at Boma, on the Congo estuary, later that afternoon.

Upstream from the city where, according to W. G. Sebald, Roger Casement had served as British Consul in the early twentieth century, its waterfront flanked by cargo ships at anchor, the river's bed narrowed and we progressed between steep hills, mostly laid bare by bush fires, some of which still glowed red, sparing only the baobabs dotted here and there among the chaos of rocks, giving the illusion of some carefully composed landscape park. Nowhere was the illusion more perfect than on the island of Libulu, small and amazingly green, its abundance of varieties of tree giving it the appearance of an arboretum.

It is, I think, at Pointe Bumbu, on the Angolan shore, that the river reaches its narrowest point on this stretch. From there on, dusk fell over the hills with their many shades of ocher and brown, giving off a strong smell of burning that reached the bridge of the *Banana Pride*, while the sky turned purple, then yellow, and finally a dull green before dark. It had been black night for over an hour when the *Banana Pride* entered the final phase of its approach, the engine on full power to counter the swirling Chaudron d'Enfer ("Hell's Cauldron"), then dropping power and speed as it passed under the suspension bridge marking the entrance to the city of Matadi, accompanied at short intervals by the singsong steering instructions issued by the pilot, dressed in a colorful print shirt bearing the image of Pope John Paul II, and finally backing up alongside a dimly lit dock that nonetheless afforded a glimpse, between the quay and the great wall of the ship's hull, of the dark, boiling waters rushing past with such force that it seemed no amount of hawsers could reduce the space between them, even with the help of a tugboat.

On a table in the officers' mess the captain had placed two bottles of Diplomat whiskey, distilled in Goa and constituting one of the most widely accepted currencies in the sea and river ports of this part of Africa, when dealing with the lower echelons of authority. Ships bring in entire cases of the stuff, only a small portion of which is intended for domestic consumption. But on seeing the two bottles, the two immigration officers indicated their displeasure and reminded the captain that he had failed to take into account their preference for cartons of L&M cigarettes, whose market value was far higher. As a result, their examination of our papers was, then, undertaken in a thoroughly bad humor. During this time, I was confined to the crew's mess, where several Filipinos were practicing their karaoke skills. The video cassettes with which they struggled to keep pace dispensed a nerve-jarring combination of pictures and music: chiefly North American students of both sexes, in casual dress, flirting and rowing around on lakes. Here, surrounded by Filipinos braying the refrains of English and American pop songs, I waited in a state of growing anxiety for the moment when the two policemen would summon me. When it came, I noticed how they fell, hungrily, on my passport, a far more interesting document to them than all the others, insofar as it testified to my intention to disembark, a situation affording them wonderfully expanded opportunities to make things difficult for me in some way. One of the two cops, more of a poseur, sharper and better informed, did his best to demolish the borrowed identity I had taken such pains to construct for the purposes of the trip, albeit under my own name. The poseur apparently thought, and quite rightly, that I could not be (as I claimed) both a professor of literature (a profession I had selected as one of the easiest for me to ape) and the representative of a commercial firm with a presence in numerous African countries, on a "fact-finding" mission. He may take me for a spy, I told myself—or maybe an undercover journalist—or he might just enjoy treating me as though I was. In an attempt to get me to drop my professorial guard, he quoted a few disjointed phrases in what he claimed was Latin, leaving me unsure as to whether I should point out their inappropriateness as a test of my literary knowledge, at the risk of annoying him, or ignore them altogether, thereby confirming his suspicions. I decided to take up the challenge, quoting other phrases—*Fortunatos nimium sua si bona norint* . . . etc.—in an arch, knowing manner, punctuating these with "hmms" and "ahs" in an attempt to appear very much at ease. But our exchange of quotations could not continue indefinitely. And when my celebrated fact-finding mission was finally brought up, I stumbled over its precise definition, and very probably assumed an air of mystery that could only make matters worse. From time to time, the Latinizing cop bent toward his colleague, keeping his eyes firmly on me all the time, to utter a few—probably unflattering—phrases in Lingala. Then he asked if I spoke the latter, as if the affair was more or less concluded. And, taking advantage of my obvious discomfort at this last question, he forced me to admit that I had spent time in the country before, although I had stated the contrary when filling in my visa application form. As soon as I pronounced the date of my last visit (I managed to keep quiet about the other two) he fixed me with a penetrating glare and slowly, lugubriously enunciated the following phrase: "That was in the time of Mobutu Sese Seko . . ." As if my visit to Zaire under the Marshall's reign made me an accomplice to his crimes, or singled me out, if not as an agent of the Marshall's reinstatement (difficult, in light of his death) then at least of the reinstatement of his partisans to all their former privilege. After this, the two cops consulted with one another again in Lingala and dismissed me without returning my passport.

By an unfortunate coincidence, they both left the ship just as the Audi was about to be winched ashore. I could see it trussed up like a camel or a cow, about to be hoisted into the air. On the quay stood a vehicle that had just undergone the same treatment, two of its tires burst from the impact of its violent landing. Despite my determination not to be identified as the owner of the car, I could not simply stand by and watch it receive the same treatment from the crane operator; I hurried down to the quayside ready to guide its landing, waving my arms and yelling. Naturally, this circus attracted the attention of the two cops, who were thereby able to establish some sort of connection between myself and the car, and discover for themselves the inaccuracy of my earlier declarations. Because even if it was (just) possible to be a professor of literature carrying out a fact-finding mission for a major commercial enterprise, it was inconceivable that this same person should be accompanying a secondhand car with a Val-de-Marne license plate. Worst of all, the two cops had almost certainly reached the entirely reasonable conclusion that I had lied about my profession and the reason for my stay in their country; but with no idea as to my motives for doing so, they surely began to suspect me of far more sinister intentions than I harbored in reality.

While the ship creaked and rocked to the rhythmic motion of the cranes on the gunwales, seizing the shipping containers and placing them on the quayside, once again I spent much of the night reading *Lost Time*, making it through to the end of *Sodom and Gomorrah*. But despite this admittedly effective antidote—transporting me to a world diametrically opposed to the one in which I found myself: a world where no one was threatened by Congolese security officers—I found it very hard to suppress the feeling that my ineptitude, amply demonstrated both during my questioning and subsequently, would lead to consequences out of all proportion to the purpose of my visit, and that things could only get worse as the information about me circulated from one official body to the next. In reality, my only consolation was the likely state of disorganization—as I saw it—of the Congolese security services as a whole, a notion nonetheless challenged by the alternative and contrary possibility, that the police were in fact the country's only properly organized, reasonably efficient bureau-cracy, as is so often the case with systems chiefly dedicated to the perpetuation of their own existence. My passport was returned with a visa stamp late the following morning, and I was invited to pay a "disembarkation tax" which no one had ever heard of. Twenty-four hours later, however, installed at the Hôtel Métropole and returning from a shopping trip, I found a note in my pigeon-hole inviting me to report to police headquarters, giving me such a scare that I might well have considered returning to the *Banana Pride* (still in dock, as I could see from my window), if that plan of action had not itself necessitated a visit to the immigration office.

The Métropole had probably been built some thirty years after Joseph Conrad's passage through Matadi. For many years it was the finest hotel in all equatorial Africa, and it still is, just about, although its comforts are more rudimentary nowadays, along the lines of the Hotel Grand in Sopot before the fall of socialism. As in all former state-run hotels, the bedrooms in the Métropole are monumentally huge, with ceilings so high that they can only have been conceived as a manifestation of the colonial Belgians' lofty sense of their own importance. In the old days, the triangular patio, overlooked by sev-eral floors of galleried landings with bedrooms leading off them, must have served as an admirable soundbox, amplifying the injunc-tions and insults hurled at the staff, whose zeal and commitment—despite rigorous training—would invariably be found wanting.

Today, that zeal had lapsed still further, and Congolese civil ser-vants were the main source of the invective directed against the lackadaisical staff, their service all the less urgent for the knowledge that the civil servants were not responsible for paying their own bills, and that these were in fact rarely settled at all. The bedroom furnishings were hideous (but happily few), the lighting intermittent and dingy, and the water available for just a few hours each day, taking ages to fill the immense bathtub, next to which stood a blue plastic bucket, just in case. But every room, or most at least, boasted an outward-facing loggia with a bay window divided by two slender columns, an architectural detail that organized the surrounding landscape into triptychs. The left panel of my own triptych framed a billboard advertising Diplomat whiskey, the "drink of the élite"; the right-hand panel afforded a view of green and russet hillsides rising in stages from the brown waters of the river; while the central panel offered a raked perspective—doubtless making the loggia a desirable vantage point in wartime—along a steep street, its disjointed paving stones slippery with sedimented trash, leading to the port security gates, and the distant panorama of installations beyond: ships in dock, cranes, hoisting gear in motion, storage sheds, workers assembled in front of the port authority offices protesting about the late arrival of their pay, disused rolling stock decomposing on railway lines overgrown with vegetation, and beyond the river, again, the pylons of the suspension bridge and the tall cliff rising above the Chaudron d'Enfer.

This was the street—half-choked throughout the day by a mass of vehicles, street traders, and pedestrians (including many who were clearly insane or infirm, mostly beggars) seething in and out through the port gates—along which I had to walk, armed with my police summons, to reach the headquarters of the company for which I was supposed to carry out my now infamous fact-finding mission.

Monsieur Kurt, the company's Matadi representative, bore no resemblance whatever to his Conradian near-namesake. Rather, his appearance suggested one of those few men of true integrity, devoid of any inclination to evil, encountered here and there in Conrad's work, their qualities all the more remarkable for being thrown into sharp relief against a background of greed, treachery, corruption, and violence. The more I observed Kurt, during the eight or ten days I spent mostly in his office, waiting for things to happen—things that he alone, in this town, as far as I knew, was able to contemplate with equanimity, and the only man likely to speed them along, in the most straightforward way possible, with no expectation of reward—the more he reminded me (still keeping to the works of Conrad) of the main character in *Victory: An Island Tale*, a skeptical adventurer who retreats to an Indonesian island to escape the chaos and disorder of the world, before it finally catches up with him there, and destroys him. Not that Kurt was the contemplative type (Heyst himself, in *Victory*, spends long years as a sailor and trader before turning his back on the world of work). But while almost everyone he dealt with in Matadi was to some degree corrupt, or merely incompetent, Kurt himself gave an impression of such utter rectitude—although he was doubtless also gifted with high cunning, and certainly capable of acting harshly in the execution of his responsibilities—that my spirits were always restored after spending time in his company, even though I knew the hospitality so generously granted in his office (he had realized just how ill at ease I felt anywhere else) would be paid for after my departure with an increased workload and frantic levels of activity. One detail, I felt, gave the measure of Kurt's character: he regularly gave money to crippled street beggars, making sure he wasn't seen, out of modesty, but also for fear of being overwhelmed with demands, and being taken for a sucker. (He had also joined a club whose members paid into a fund to buy food for inmates at Matadi Prison—without this, they had nothing to eat—but put an end to the same when he found that all of the money had been embezzled away.) Kurt first intervened to get me out of a tight spot by sending his personnel director to the police in my stead, confirming that my status as a consultant (in the context of the fact-finding mission) placed me under the company's protection for as long as I remained in the country. No further summons was forthcoming after that. Next, he saw to a welter of administrative procedures of such sinuous complexity that I lost their thread completely, ultimately leading to the release of the Audi, which had been sequestered earlier in a section of the port closed to public access.

Meanwhile Foudron's two emissaries, Nsele and Patrice, had arrived in Matadi. Both immediately demonstrated their lack of even the most rudimentary knowledge of the proper procedure for taking delivery of an imported vehicle. I met them for the first time in the small triangular courtyard dotted with tables and chairs, at the bottom of the Hotel Métropole's central well. It seemed to me that Nsele talked a great deal but said nothing, putting on a show of optimism bordering on the incantational ("Tomorrow night we will be in Kinshasa!" and so forth), and apparently calculated to absolve him of responsibility in the event of any difficulties encountered along the way. As for Patrice, his natural reticence was compounded by the fact that he spoke very little French, this at least having the advantage of making him appear far more thoughtful, reasonable, and trustworthy than Nsele.

In the days that followed—while acknowledging that I neither should nor could involve myself in any way at all with the affair, being officially completely unconnected with the car—I made efforts, operating chiefly out of Kurt's office, and with his help, to guide Nsele (who had taken sole charge of this portion of the paperwork, Patrice having been designated exclusively as our mechanic and driver) through the arcana of a procedure to which we were both completely new, and which I sometimes suspected him of deliberately enriching with additional administrative flourishes designed to procure some further small personal advantage. In fact, Patrice and Nsele were intervening in this process purely in their capacity as intermediaries mandated by Foudron's wife Clémentine, the ultimate recipient of the car and the revenues from its eventual operation as a taxi. To all intents and purposes, then, Nsele had no personal interest in the outcome of the affair, although Clémentine had doubtless promised him some payment in the event of a successful conclusion. Patrice, for his part, would be the taxi driver once the Audi had completed its transformation, and would, in this capacity, receive a percentage of its income. As the days went by, I made stringent efforts to avoid coming into direct contact with Nsele (who nonetheless petitioned me for extra funding in the face of each new or imagined difficulty), and felt myself overcome by a creeping sense of lassitude or indifference such that I was even tempted to abandon the whole business and disappear. The sheer size of the country, and its chaotic state, seemed highly propitious in this regard, but my hopes of escape were undermined by the scarcity and precariousness of every means of transport, and the number of checkpoints and tolls to which these were subject. Hence I spent whole days in Kurt's office—he busying himself with innumerable tasks (for the most part consisting of nothing but the patient removal of obstacles surreptitiously put in place by the authorities or some other agent, in order to levy unwarranted taxes on the flow of goods and merchandise), me sitting sideways on a chair, sometimes silent but more often ready to chat, watching the endless procession of petitioners, lawyers, intermediaries, clients, or company employees staggering under bulging files full of papers needing to be stamped and signed. From my vantage point, I could see not only the port, whose frenzied activity reinforced my belief that the car would never emerge from its confines, but also the eddying flow of the river, glimpsed beyond the rooftops of the storage sheds, its opposite bank dominated by green and ocher hills.

One day, Kurt took me to lunch at the Ledia, one of Matadi's best-known and well-regarded hotels. The parking lot featured two cages, one containing a chimpanzee clearly harboring a bitter grudge against humankind in general, to whom he exhibited his emunctory orifices at every opportunity, and the other a monkey of a smaller, calmer species with a very long tail and a black tuft on the top of its head. The parking lot was separated from the hotel's terrace by a wall with a gate for the use of pedestrians or service vehicles only. The terrace itself was shaded by palm trees and decked with flowering hibiscus shrubs. After lunch, as I lingered on the terrace after Kurt had returned to his office, the security guard in charge of the parking lot stepped out of his own territory and ventured into mine, that of the hotel's clientele, to ask me for a cigarette, thereby infringing at least two of the rules governing the behavior of hotel staff. The security guard was a young man of suitably athletic build, dressed in black military fatigues and black combat boots. He may also have sported a black cap, and a truncheon in his belt. Seeing him leave his post on the parking lot to march straight across the open space, through the gateway and toward me, I wondered for a moment if he intended to knock me out. There are some circumstances in which no one can keep from making such suppositions. And now the security guard was talking to me, perhaps to mitigate the impropriety of his approach, or perhaps because he just felt like talking once his cigarette was lit, rather than heading straight back to roast on the parking lot tarmac, which was in any case completely devoid of cars. In return for my gift of a cigarette (although I could scarcely be said to have had a choice in the matter), he told me how highly he thought of the French, and how their colonial endeavors were far superior to those of the Belgians. As proof of the superiority of French-style colonization, he cited the level of development in Congo-Brazzaville (as he called it), which was indeed, for the moment, higher than that in the Democratic Republic, even though few Congolese reaped the benefits, and the precise role of French colonization in that country's increasing oil revenues remained largely unclear. "The French can live with African people," the security guard insisted, "but the Belgians cannot." And of course, although I have nothing against Belgians, unlike W. G. Sebald, I was careful not to dispute this idea, venturing at most to point out that the development of the Congo (Kinshasa) should be, above all, a project for the Congolese themselves (I was taking no chances). The security guard agreed; he was, I began to feel, a likeable man, animated by genuine patriotic feeling, expressed in terms other than the familiar swaggering pronouncements and anathemas.

"Nowadays," the security guard went on, "with the transitional government, everyone is helping themselves to some extent" (by which he meant that many people were busy lining their own pockets). But after the elections—the ones which had just been postponed and were now scheduled for the following year—the security guard hoped that under the authority of a "democratically elected" president the country would get to work and build, first and foremost, a strong army to "guarantee security," which had diminished considerably after the trampling and pillaging it had suffered in recent years. Perhaps he also hoped to become an officer in that army, one day. Listening to him, with the near certainty that his hopes would be dashed, and that no good would come of the elections, if they ever took place at all—although I refrained from saying so—I wondered why no state in Africa, at least among those of which I had personal knowledge, was capable, or, probably, even desirous of making good use of the qualities of a man like him.

On Friday September 9, quite suddenly, just before noon, the Audi left the port area and found itself almost immediately on the forecourt of the headquarters of the regional tax authority. I caught up with it just as its license plates were being changed. Then, with Patrice at the wheel, we headed for a retread shop located near the Vodaphone traffic circle—named for a billboard dominating its central traffic island, cell-phone ads having invaded every corner of the country's public space, largely supplanting the signs for various brands of beer—and just below a police station that looked to me to be the largest and best equipped in the whole of Matadi. Kurt had joined us there, stopping on the way to greet a man in the street who turned out to be the captain of the *Luanda Bridge*, a ship serving the same line as the *Banana Pride*, and who was, for the moment at least, still unaware that he had just lost his job, following an incident in which he (or his First Mate—this was a matter of some dispute) had struck a prostitute and knocked out her client in a barroom brawl.

Nsele, who had vanished after the changing of the plates, reappeared at the retread shop with his and Patrice's bags. Half an hour later, after some last minute tuning-up (which subsequent events were to prove wholly inadequate), the car rolled out of Matadi, preceded by Kurt's 4x4, in the direction of the M'poso Bridge. The entrance to the latter was barred by a series of roadblocks that it was impossible to pass without some form of assistance. (Any vehicle entering the narrow passage leading to the bridge was immediately assailed by generally obese women dressed in yellow shirts with gold buttons and sporting metal helmets in the same color, doing their best to prevent said vehicle from moving forward, in order to extract payment of outlandish fines from its driver, all of which was as nothing to what lay ahead at the entrance to the bridge itself, where the vehicle would be attacked from all sides by the representatives of various constituent bodies, quickly finding itself in a situation comparable to that of a rugby ball at the heart of a scrum.)

Beyond the bridge, Kurt accompanied us for another few kilometers before turning back. At times, the road along which we now drove, between high hills stripped of vegetation, followed the route of the railway lines whose construction had led to the deaths of so many men. It was through these same hills that Conrad had travelled, one hundred and fifteen years earlier, accompanied by thirty-one porters and the aforementioned Prosper Harou, whose nationality was apparently not French, but Belgian. For almost one hundred kilometers, everything went well, although Patrice was twice forced to stop and look under the hood, at the overheating engine, where he saw nothing untoward. And each one of us—with good reason it now seemed—was congratulating himself that we would reach Kinshasa that very evening, when the radiator hose burst.

My arrival in the capital, at the end of the journey interrupted for some hours by the explosion of the radiator hose, coincided with a major international congress of experts on the great apes. Apart from making a number of important decisions—all fated to pass unnoticed, given that people who lack every basic necessity, people who are being hunted by troops threatening to exterminate them, and then the troops themselves, and sometimes even the international forces deployed to contain the troops' brutality, none could give a damn for the protection of the great apes, finding it far more profitable (if ever they came across any) to eat them or sell them—the congress demonstrated the generous spirit, or short memories, of great ape specialists as a whole, given that four of their colleagues had been abducted and held captive for a lengthy period of time (thirty years earlier, admittedly) by Laurent-Désiré Kabila, the father of the current head of state and the man who had brought down Mobutu and subsequently reigned over the Congo (formerly Zaire) in his turn for almost four years, until his assassination on January 16, 2001. (And since it had been slightly more than four years, on my arrival in Kinshasa, since Kabila Senior had been succeeded by Joseph Kabila, it could fairly be said that the son had already improved on his father's record by a few months.)

In my capacity as a consultant hired by a powerful company to carry out an important fact-finding mission, I should have descended on the Memling, or any one of Kinshasa's other international hotels. But I chose to stay at a more modest establishment instead, the Protestant Welcome Center. Its clientele consisted mostly of amiable, smiling ministers of the church who maintained a discreet, often silent presence when not presiding over their religious services. The decor suited me just as well as the clientele: single-story huts in sober, military style, with sparse greenery and dusty ground between. My only concern was that if I attracted the police's curiosity once again, they were unlikely to be so naïve as to fail to notice the glaring disparity between my choice of accommodations and my professional cover. All of which was made more absurd still by the fact that, essentially, I had nothing whatever to hide, at least nothing that could be interpreted as a threat to the security of the Congolese State, and that I had declared to my nonexistent mission solely in order to obtain a visa.

The Protestant Welcome Center overlooked Avenue de Kalemie, not far from the intersection with Avenue Longole Lutete. These topographical indications are of only limited use, because Kinshasa is one of those cities where no one calls a street by its current name.

Avenue de Kalemie runs parallel and very close to the riverbank, with several dead-end streets leading off it, toward the water's edge. The city's riverfront is occupied along its entire length by port infrastructures or office buildings, military zones, and the residences of official dignitaries, in ascending order of privacy and inaccessibility. So that the waterfront, and the sight of the river, which should constitute one of the chief attractions in a city with all too few to its name, is almost entirely closed off to the public. (During my stay in Kinshasa, I was free to contemplate the river, the islands of the Malebo Pool, and the silhouette of the tall buildings in Brazzaville on the opposite bank only once— although my vantage point and pretext, if they had been discovered, would have been likely, once again, to confirm the charge of espionage, my fear of which was rapidly becoming something of an obsession. The view was afforded by a visit to the upper floors of the Forescom building, some of which stood empty, crowning a sort of architectural wasteland extending over several stories and, in places, overgrown with weeds—once one of the most luxurious buildings in Kinshasa, and now one of its finest inhabited ruins). The day I checked into the Protestant Welcome Center, I decided to take an evening stroll up Avenue de Kalemie in the direction of the house that had, at various times, been my father's residence, forty years earlier, and where I myself had lived two or three times. I had hardly set foot outside the Center's front gate when I committed my first faux pas, heading down one of the dead-end streets leading to the river to take a closer look at a pair of Gray Gabon parrots I had spotted, thanks to their loud cawing, in a tree whose fruit they were now eating. There were no barriers or signs forbidding entry to the street, and I saw a large number of people leaving it on foot, doubtless on their way home from work. But while I stood in rapt contemplation of the pair of parrots, a soldier in a green beret—probably singling him out as a member of some elite corps—stepped out of a dark shadow, where I had failed to notice him, walked over to me, and told me that it was forbidden to walk down the dead-end street, or even to look at it, a ruling that at least twenty people were currently infringing at that same moment, before his very eyes. He then waited a few moments, arms swinging, before adding without looking me directly in the eye, that he "needed a little taste of sugar . . ." I gave him two hundred Congolese francs (in other words, almost nothing) and he returned to his post in the dark corner where I had failed to spot him. Incidents such as this were not about to bring me to the brink of financial ruin, no matter how often they were repeated, nor were they particularly shocking, given that the country's soldiers were almost never paid their due. But it seemed to me that these incessant demands were as humiliating for the person delivering the hand-out as they were for the recipient, especially if the latter was wearing a uniform and exercised some small amount of authority. Other uniformed types, with no official power whatever, were to be found in front of every gateway along Avenue de Kalemie. These men, ordinary security guards, were generally friendly and less inclined to make demands, their lack of official power making them more vulnerable than the military to a refusal. But there was an appalling hopelessness, too, in the belief they all shared, to varying degrees, that any easily approachable white man—approachable because momentarily deprived of his protective automobile armor—was capable of changing their lives, either by securing them a better job, or by helping them to leave the country altogether. As I continued in the direction of what some street maps of Kinshasa call "Promenade de la Roquette"—although to the best of my knowledge, no one has ever heard it called anything of the kind—the light dwindled, and it was almost dark when I passed in front of a decrepit villa surrounded by lines of barbed wire in which I thought I recognized the former residence of the French ambassador, the house where I had watched Marshall Mobutu and the future Emperor Bokasa step inside, the latter leaning on a white cane and sporting a lustrous, sleek fur hat. The new ambassador's residence had been built a little farther along, doubtless in the 1980s, because I had no recollection of having seen it before. The villa once inhabited by my father, on the corner of Avenue de Kalemenie and Avenue Lilas, looked unchanged from the outside, even down to the openwork wall separating it from the street, which its present occupant had neither raised nor reinforced, unlike most of his neighbors, whose homes were solidly retrenched. This not-insignificant detail alone reflected a proud tradition to which my father had contributed (to the extent that when the city's French Cultural Center was sacked by rioters in the late 1960s—rioters he suspected, characteristically, of being manipulated by the Americans—far from feeling angry or upset, he had simply posted a sign at the entrance to the vandalized premises indicating that they would remain closed "for the duration of the popular festivities"). The openwork perimeter wall afforded views of the garden, also unchanged, insofar as I could remember its features—the water basin inhabited, back then, by a kingfisher who would swoop low to fly over it, back and forth, every evening.

Night fell as I stood looking at the house. Continuing on my way, I reached the point where Avenue de Kalemie joins the river, and found myself confronting another soldier in combat fatigues: this one, at my approach, had emerged from a bolt-hole where he stood sheltered behind a parapet of sandbags. The installation testified to the strategic importance of the place he was protecting, about which I naturally refrained from asking, judging that the simple fact of wandering on foot in the dark near the site, whatever it was, would be enough in any country, let alone this one, to prompt a whole host of suspicions supporting an accusation not only of espionage but also sabotage, or attempted sabotage, such as the one I had attracted in 1980 at the airport in Kisangani. But while the man who arrested me in Kisangani was a small-time hustler, accredited (or not) with one or other of the security services, the soldier emerging from his hole was apparently of a more philanthropic outlook, or a patriot of the same ilk as the security guard at the parking lot in Matadi. He was content simply to examine my passport under his flashlight, and notify me that it was forbidden to walk any farther in the same direction, before disappearing into his hole again, making no demands. He had, nonetheless, checked—if not taken particular note of—my identity in a place where I clearly shouldn't have been found wandering at all.

The next day, I learned the reason for the riverbank's inaccessibility: it was the location of Jean-Pierre Bemba's home; Bemba being one of the four associate vice presidents forming the head of the government under Joseph Kabila.* Jean-Pierre Bemba is also the son-in-law of Marshal Mobutu, and the son of one of the men who profited most from an alliance with the latter: under the reign of Laurent-Désiré Kabila, however, Bemba Senior (known as Jeannot) rallied to the new régime while Bemba Junior (Jean-Pierre) dabbled in business in Europe. In 1998, when Kabila's former Rwandan and Ugandan allies turned against him, Jean-Pierre Bemba was persuaded to establish a guerilla movement, the MLC (Mouvement de libération du Congo), whose troops were in large part composed of veterans of the FAZ (the Forces Armées Zaïroises). All this requires a certain effort to understand, admittedly: but it is not my fault, nor that of any single individual—with the possible exception of Leopold II—if the recent history of the Congo is so complicated. With the support of the Ugandans (but no longer the Rwandans, who now had other irons in the fire), the MLC scored several early successes (if they can be called such) in Bemba's native eastern province, before establishing a solid base in another province, Équateur (Mobutu's homeland, where he still enjoyed strong support). Équateur also shares a border with the Central African Republic, where MLC troops would later intervene alongside a Libyan contingent, to support President Ange-Félix Patassé in the face of an attempted coup. All of this in no way prevented Jean-Pierre Bemba from doing excellent business with

---

* Almost exactly a year later, a tank maneuvered by soldiers in the pay of Joseph Kabila presented itself at the entrance to this villa—when the entire diplomatic community was gathered inside—and proceeded to fire at and destroy the helicopter that Jean-Pierre Bemba kept on standby, just in case, in his garden.

his Ugandan protectors (gold, diamonds, wood, coffee etc.). By the terms of the Pretoria Agreement, signed in December 2002, instituting a "transitional government" in Kinshasa, in the expectation of hypothetical elections, Joseph Kabila (Junior) was confirmed as President of the Republic, with Jean-Pierre Bemba as one of the four vice presidents. This promotion failed to silence the accusations of war crimes leveled against his movement, involving (to take just one example) atrocities carried out against the Pygmies in the Ituri River basin. In this region, elements of the MLC are suspected not only of having massacred the Pygmies, but of carrying out acts of cannibalism on some of their victims.

To counter these accusations, Jean-Pierre Bemba organized an exhibition of nine Pygmies in September 2004, on the stage of the Grand Hôtel in Kinshasa, "dressed," said a news agency dispatch, "in new suits that the tailor had not had time to adjust to their size."

"The Pygmies of Mambasa," the dispatch went on (this same phrase was also its title), "declared that they had not been eaten."

Among Clémentine's photographs of her husband, one recent picture shows him in his security guard's uniform—black jacket and tie, white shirt—standing behind the counter in the La Fourche McDonald's in Paris. Another older, slightly overexposed picture shows him dressed in camouflage fatigues, wearing combat boots and a black beret, emerging with other officers of the FAZ from the hold of a C-130 (a troop transport plane), its propellers still turning. Clémentine doesn't remember where the photograph was taken: the aerodrome at Kisangani? Lubumbashi? Goma? She counts off the list of towns and cities to which she followed Foudron, as an officer's wife: garrison to garrison. Among other likeable traits, possibly distinguishing Foudron from numerous other military men serving in the FAZ at the same period, she cites his love of cooking, and his eagerness to cook, not without talent, when they invited friends over. She talks about the period when he stopped smoking, and about his mother whose portrait hangs in the sitting room, wearing a colorful shift dress printed with the image of the Virgin Mary. Simple family souvenirs. No reference to Foudron's record of service. Regarding her husband's exile in Europe, Clémentine knows no reason for it other than his poor health, and the need to secure appropriate treatment for his heart condition. She doesn't seem overly curious about his life in Paris, about which I myself know very little. The two daughters, one of whom has just taken her baccalaureate, or the local equivalent of a baccalaureate, show the same diffidence, while also expressing great enthusiasm for their father, and his photographs. During the meal, our conversation continues in the same innocuous, familial vein. As is almost always the case in Africa, a whole portion of the household only appears at irregular intervals, standing aside in the kitchen or outside on the yard of beaten earth, beneath the lines of floating laundry, hung out to dry.

Nsele comes to dinner, but Patrice excuses himself, returning at the wheel of the Audi just a few minutes before it's time to leave. The eldest girl, the one who has just taken her baccalaureate, expresses a desire to study law while at the same perfecting her sewing skills, because, as she observes, there is no way of knowing whether there will be plenty of work for lawyers in the Congo in the future, whereas there will always be work for a seamstress. "Even in wartime," she adds, giving some measure of the extent of her optimism. Indeed, on the previous night, a service station in a nearby neighborhood was attacked by uniformed soldiers, this time exchanging fire with the police. As always, the account of the affair in the press is calculated to shed no light on it whatsoever. Today, state schoolteachers, unpaid for several months, are threatening to take to the streets with their pupils, as a result of which the country's private schools have also taken the day off, fearing attacks on their staff and clientele by the strikers.

I steer the conversation to the subject of street children, many of whom have apparently been chased out by their families on suspicion of witchcraft; Clémentine is shocked by such attitudes, but doesn't question the possibility that the children may indeed be bewitched, or witches themselves. The same goes for the eldest daughter, who tells how a man who had stolen a cell phone was recently killed by remote control, by the owner of the stolen item, who had appeared on its screen several times beforehand, issuing warnings to the thief that the latter had ignored (the screens of cell phones, and TV screens too, were also the medium of choice for dead people making contact with the living). None of this was in question, she added, although her fervent Catholicism lead her to make it clear that the sorcerers' powers were limited, even neg-ligible, by comparison with those of "Almighty God." Before the meal, everyone had stood up to say grace.

Patrice's reappearance is the sign that it was time to leave. Parked in front of the "compound"—the patch of earth on which the house was built, surrounded by a cement block wall—the Audi sparkles like new (every morning, Patrice pays a tiny sum of money to a street child, who washes it from top to bottom). The radiator still has a tendency to boil over, however.

On the way back, Patrice wants to give me a demonstration of how taxis operate in Kinshasa, where they are in such short supply that any vehicle can, at any moment, permanently or otherwise, be converted into a means of public transport, usually operating—as would the buses, if they existed—along a regular line, such as the drag leading from Place de la Victoire to Place du Marché and the central station. At the intersection with Avenue Pierre Mulele and Avenue Monseigneur Kimbondo, one of the hubs of this informal network, the crowd of postulants is too dense, too uneasy, and Patrice chooses not to stop. Just ahead of us, some men in military fatigues seem to be seizing a Volkswagen Combi by force, emptying it of its passengers. A little further along, near the Palais du Peuple, the Audi takes on board a woman with a pockmarked face, heading for the vicinity of the central station. Throughout the journey, her two cell phones ring incessantly at the bottom of her bag, and she answers each of them in turn. We are now five in the car—Patrice, Nsele, the eldest daughter, the woman with the pockmarked face, and me—but potential clients continue to present themselves whenever we slow down, turning away when they see us. They are dissuaded from climbing aboard, says the eldest daughter, by the presence of a white man inside the car, because there is a rumor that Europeans, working with Congolese associates, are currently plying the streets of Kinshasa looking for organs to harvest. When the woman with the two cell phones gets out of the car unscathed near the central station, she presents Patrice with two ragged notes (one hundred Congolese francs apiece), the only transaction I am given to witness, attesting to the Audi's transformation into a taxi.

Every time I suggested to Patrice that he drive me to the Kinsuka Rapids, he would reply that the surrounding area had become too dangerous. But I wondered if the same response might not have been forthcoming had I expressed a wish to see the Coliseum, for example, or Times Square, concealing his ignorance of the Rapids' very existence, or at best how to get there. If I insisted, Patrice would maintain that people had been taken captive there— although there was no way of knowing whether their captors were soldiers, or gang members, or soldiers acting on behalf of gangs, or vice versa—and possibly accused of spying. There was some logic to this: I remembered that the river was especially narrow along this stretch, so that the opposite bank, the other Congo, was very close. Strangely, none of the people I questioned on this subject had ever been to the Rapids, and the mystery surrounding this natural wonder was such that I began to wonder whether they truly existed, under that name at least, or whether I had completely fabricated the episode in which Conrad is nearly wrecked there, in a rowing boat, narrowly escaping the loss of both his life and the manuscript of *Almayer's Folly*. Perhaps, I told myself, I had imagined the episode as a result of some subconscious desire to kill Conrad off before the publication of his first book (to nip him in the bud). As for the rapids, they really exist, under the name I gave them, or a different one, because I clearly remembered going to see them in the 1960s, under my own steam, no less, at the wheel of a Renault 4L, the only vehicle I have ever succeeded in mastering. But perhaps this was a complete fabrication too, like my claim to have worked for the secret service in the past. Or like Foudron's story about how he crossed the river in a rickety boat, under cover of darkness, to seek refuge in Brazzaville.

There was no doubt, however, that Patrice had spent several years fighting in Angola on one side or the other, not out of conviction, but necessity, either because he was enlisted by force or more probably because he had found no better way of earning a living at the time. Indeed, he retained a certain nostalgia for his army days. I even heard him maintain, perhaps with a hint of irony, that he would like to see a war start again in his country, with all the get-rich-quick opportunities such campaigns afforded for its combatants, as they had done for so long, and on such a great scale, in Angola, giving the Cubans the opportunity of a dazzling military victory (at Cuito Canavale) and obliterating, to some extent, the memory of Che Guevara's African failures. On this subject, and during the same conversation, around a wobbly table on the sidewalk of Boulevard 30 Juin, at nightfall, Patrice told me how the group of combatants to which he had belonged regularly used *dawa*. He still believed in its efficacy—contrary to all evidence, it seemed to me—because when the vehicle he was driving hit a landmine, all the other occupants had been killed (despite splashing themselves with *dawa* beforehand, like him). But Patrice remained convinced that he owed his personal salvation to the *dawa* and nothing else. Even when he talked of war, or his desire to return to it, he showed the same immense calm, the same kind and gentle manner, although this impression was perhaps due to the fact that his words were simultaneously translated for me by Nsele. Both drank a great deal of beer. But this was nothing compared to the quantities already drunk by the customer at the next table, accompanied by two probable prostitutes, flailing about in the midst of empty bottles of Skol, declaring that "the whites will do whatever they want with this country, no worries." The diatribe may have been directed at me personally, and the impunity I continued to enjoy in my activities as a spy (or saboteur). As for all the rest, it wasn't only whites, nor even all whites, whose crimes and misdemeanors had gone unpunished, but anyone with the means to pay up, or otherwise curry favor with the authorities. My own impunity was not, it seemed, fated to last much longer, particularly if Patrice—not content to present me with almost daily bills for improbable fines or pointless repairs to the Audi, such as the fitting of a bigger radiator, which would be slower to boil, when it was clearly the cylinder head gasket that needed replacing—were to become involved in an accident resulting in significant damage to the car, other property, himself, or other people, forcing him (in the face of the immense reparations that were certain to be demanded) to incriminate me, no matter how much I liked him, or he me, by informing on me as the importer of the car and blowing my cover as a business consultant.

I now feared being thrown into prison as the result of a traffic accident far more than the charge of espionage, which had now been too long in coming to remain plausible. In the crash scenario, even the company providing me with my cover would be powerless to help, aside from putting me in touch with a lawyer. In addition to which, sometime around September 20, I finished reading *The Prisoner*, and without really being able to say why, it seemed impossible to start on *The Fugitive* right away (partly, perhaps, because of all the episodes in *Lost Time*, *The Prisoner* is the one in which the narrator appears in the least positive light). And with the television in my bedroom out of action, I now had nothing to do in the evening except drag my chair to the door and crush mosquitoes while gazing at the papaya tree sprouting from a corner of the cement-block perimeter wall, above which, at dusk, I could see flocks of parrots and white egrets against the green sky, the former flying faster and more noisily than the latter. After this, I would take dinner in the refectory, in the company of single men whom I took, rightly or wrongly, to be Protestant ministers, although thinking about it I cannot remember seeing them at prayer, or showing an interest in anything other than football.

And so, as the days went by, my reasons for remaining in Kinshasa became increasingly tenuous, and my reasons for leaving more and more pressing. After mid-September, and particularly in light of the difficulty of getting around town or the surrounding area due to the checkpoints set at every street corner by officers in the yellow shirts of the *roulage* (an old Belgian term for the traffic police), and the uncertainty besetting my various schemes, my stay was turning into little more than a form of house arrest within the confines of the Protestant Welcome Center. My inactivity also made my cover as a business consultant less and less plausible. And, inexorably, I was running out of money. Shortly after September 20 (with the final, innocuous words of *The Prisoner* still echoing in my head), I decided to go home. My decision was both hasty and irreversible: as soon as it was taken, every extra day spent in Kinshasa seemed like one day too many.

I lived in dread of an accident involving the car, which would inevitably draw me into a steep downward spiral—a veritable maelstrom—of hassles and difficulties. Besides which, my business in the city was truly at an end: if the car was indeed to become a taxi, the family now had everything they needed—except perhaps, for the moment, a cylinder head gasket—to make a success of the business. And if they had other uses for it mind—selling it for ready cash, for example—my continued presence would only be a source of embarrassment. In order to leave the country, I had to visit the French embassy to offload certain documents that proved nothing against me, but which I nonetheless preferred not to fall into the hands of the police during the inevitable checks at the airport. And it was while running this errand—after spending part of the morning in the bar of the Hôtel Memling, and experiencing once again the difficulty of getting around the city on foot, having been pursued by a street child for an hour, and then by a horde of the same, tirelessly chanting the refrain "street child, street child," despite my attempts to divert their attention to the diplomats or wealthy Congolese in their Mercedes, crawling past in the slow-moving traffic; having finally reached the shelter of the embassy compound, and loitering in its corridors for a while, looking for a person whose name had been indicated to me—that suddenly, there, through a half-open door, I thought I recognized the office my father had occupied in the 1960s, almost unchanged since my last visit, in 1980. And it must have been here, in this office—although he also, I presume, spent plenty of time just opposite, in the bar of the Hôtel Memling, or other places in Kinshasa unknown to me and probably long since vanished—that my father had received, by telegram or some other means, telephone communications having been momentarily interrupted, the urgent message sent by my mother from Paris at the end of May 1968, informing him that I had just been hospitalized in critical condition.

As a result of which, according to a family legend that I can no longer substantiate, imagining me to be the victim of police brutality, my father had decided, in the event of my death, to solicit an interview with the French Minister of the Interior—a boon he could easily obtain, in his capacity as a former Gaullist, especially in this context—in the course of which he planned to assassinate said Minister using an American 11.43 mm caliber pistol, which he had kept, but taken no care of whatsoever, since the end of the war. One may easily imagine the turn of "the Events" if such a chain of circumstances had indeed come to pass. The Trois Glorieuses and June Days Uprising would have been as nothing. I should tell that story one day—the story of my heroic death, and the revolution that ensued.

JEAN ROLIN is a French writer and journalist, the winner of the 1988 Albert Londres Prize for journalism, and the 1996 Prix Médicis for his novel *L'organisation*. As a student, he was closely involved—along with his older brother Olivier (author of *Hotel Crystal*)—in the May '68 uprising. He is the author of essays, novels, and short stories. In 2006, his nonfiction collection *L'homme qui a vu l'ours* won the Prix Ptolémée.

LOUISE ROGERS LALAURIE is a translator, writer, and editor based near Paris. She studied English, literary translation, and art history at Queen's College, Cambridge, and was a magazine journalist and book editor before moving to France, where she translates for the Ministry of Culture, the Louvre, and other leading museums and distributions.

SELECTED DALKEY ARCHIVE PAPERBACKS

PETROS ABATZOGLOU, *What Does Mrs. Freeman Want?*
MICHAL AJVAZ, *The Golden Age.*
The Other City.
PIERRE ALBERT-BIROT, *Grabinoulor.*
YUZ ALESHKOVSKY, *Kangaroo.*
FELIPE ALFAU, *Chromos.*
Locos.
IVAN ÂNGELO, *The Celebration.*
The Tower of Glass.
DAVID ANTIN, *Talking.*
ANTÓNIO LOBO ANTUNES, *Knowledge of Hell.*
ALAIN ARIAS-MISSON, *Theatre of Incest.*
IFTIKHAR ARIF AND WAQAS KHWAJA, EDS., *Modern Poetry of Pakistan.*
JOHN ASHBERY AND JAMES SCHUYLER, *A Nest of Ninnies.*
GABRIELA AVIGUR-ROTEM, *Heatwave and Crazy Birds.*
HEIMRAD BÄCKER, *transcript.*
DJUNA BARNES, *Ladies Almanack.*
Ryder.
JOHN BARTH, *LETTERS.*
Sabbatical.
DONALD BARTHELME, *The King.*
Paradise.
SVETISLAV BASARA, *Chinese Letter.*
RENÉ BELLETTO, *Dying.*
MARK BINELLI, *Sacco and Vanzetti Must Die!*
ANDREI BITOV, *Pushkin House.*
ANDREJ BLATNIK, *You Do Understand.*
LOUIS PAUL BOON, *Chapel Road.*
My Little War.
Summer in Termuren.
ROGER BOYLAN, *Killoyle.*
IGNÁCIO DE LOYOLA BRANDÃO, *Anonymous Celebrity.*
The Good-Bye Angel.
Teeth under the Sun.
Zero.
BONNIE BREMSER, *Troia: Mexican Memoirs.*
CHRISTINE BROOKE-ROSE, *Amalgamemnon.*
BRIGID BROPHY, *In Transit.*
MEREDITH BROSNAN, *Mr. Dynamite.*
GERALD L. BRUNS, *Modern Poetry and the Idea of Language.*
EVGENY BUNIMOVICH AND J. KATES, EDS., *Contemporary Russian Poetry: An Anthology.*
GABRIELLE BURTON, *Heartbreak Hotel.*
MICHEL BUTOR, *Degrees.*
Mobile.
Portrait of the Artist as a Young Ape.
G. CABRERA INFANTE, *Infante's Inferno.*
Three Trapped Tigers.
JULIETA CAMPOS, *The Fear of Losing Eurydice.*
ANNE CARSON, *Eros the Bittersweet.*
ORLY CASTEL-BLOOM, *Dolly City.*
CAMILO JOSÉ CELA, *Christ versus Arizona.*
The Family of Pascual Duarte.
The Hive.
LOUIS-FERDINAND CÉLINE, *Castle to Castle.*
Conversations with Professor Y.
London Bridge.
Normance.

North.
Rigadoon.
HUGO CHARTERIS, *The Tide Is Right.*
JEROME CHARYN, *The Tar Baby.*
ERIC CHEVILLARD, *Demolishing Nisard.*
MARC CHOLODENKO, *Mordechai Schamz.*
JOSHUA COHEN, *Witz.*
EMILY HOLMES COLEMAN, *The Shutter of Snow.*
ROBERT COOVER, *A Night at the Movies.*
STANLEY CRAWFORD, *Log of the S.S. The Mrs Unguentine.*
Some Instructions to My Wife.
ROBERT CREELEY, *Collected Prose.*
RENÉ CREVEL, *Putting My Foot in It.*
RALPH CUSACK, *Cadenza.*
SUSAN DAITCH, *L.C.*
Storytown.
NICHOLAS DELBANCO, *The Count of Concord.*
Sherbrookes.
NIGEL DENNIS, *Cards of Identity.*
PETER DIMOCK, *A Short Rhetoric for Leaving the Family.*
ARIEL DORFMAN, *Konfidenz.*
COLEMAN DOWELL, *The Houses of Children.*
Island People.
Too Much Flesh and Jabez.
ARKADII DRAGOMOSHCHENKO, *Dust.*
RIKKI DUCORNET, *The Complete Butcher's Tales.*
The Fountains of Neptune.
The Jade Cabinet.
The One Marvelous Thing.
Phosphor in Dreamland.
The Stain.
The Word "Desire."
WILLIAM EASTLAKE, *The Bamboo Bed.*
Castle Keep.
Lyric of the Circle Heart.
JEAN ECHENOZ, *Chopin's Move.*
STANLEY ELKIN, *A Bad Man.*
Boswell: A Modern Comedy.
Criers and Kibitzers, Kibitzers and Criers.
The Dick Gibson Show.
The Franchiser.
George Mills.
The Living End.
The MacGuffin.
The Magic Kingdom.
Mrs. Ted Bliss.
The Rabbi of Lud.
Van Gogh's Room at Arles.
ANNIE ERNAUX, *Cleaned Out.*
LAUREN FAIRBANKS, *Muzzle Thyself.*
Sister Carrie.
LESLIE A. FIEDLER, *Love and Death in the American Novel.*
JUAN FILLOY, *Op Oloop.*
GUSTAVE FLAUBERT, *Bouvard and Pécuchet.*
KASS FLEISHER, *Talking out of School.*
FORD MADOX FORD, *The March of Literature.*
JON FOSSE, *Aliss at the Fire.*
Melancholy.
MAX FRISCH, *I'm Not Stiller.*
Man in the Holocene.

SELECTED DALKEY ARCHIVE PAPERBACKS

CARLOS FUENTES, *Christopher Unborn.*
  Distant Relations.
  Terra Nostra.
  Where the Air Is Clear.
JANICE GALLOWAY, *Foreign Parts.*
  The Trick Is to Keep Breathing.
WILLIAM H. GASS, *Cartesian Sonata*
  and Other Novellas.
  Finding a Form.
  A Temple of Texts.
  The Tunnel.
  Willie Masters' Lonesome Wife.
GÉRARD GAVARRY, *Hoppla! 1 2 3.*
  Making a Novel.
ETIENNE GILSON,
  The Arts of the Beautiful.
  Forms and Substances in the Arts.
C. S. GISCOMBE, *Giscome Road.*
  Here.
  Prairie Style.
DOUGLAS GLOVER, *Bad News of the Heart.*
  The Enamoured Knight.
WITOLD GOMBROWICZ,
  A Kind of Testament.
KAREN ELIZABETH GORDON,
  The Red Shoes.
GEORGI GOSPODINOV, *Natural Novel.*
JUAN GOYTISOLO, *Count Julian.*
  Exiled from Almost Everywhere.
  Juan the Landless.
  Makbara.
  Marks of Identity.
PATRICK GRAINVILLE, *The Cave of Heaven.*
HENRY GREEN, *Back.*
  Blindness.
  Concluding.
  Doting.
  Nothing.
JIŘÍ GRUŠA, *The Questionnaire.*
GABRIEL GUDDING,
  Rhode Island Notebook.
MELA HARTWIG, *Am I a Redundant*
  Human Being?
JOHN HAWKES, *The Passion Artist.*
  Whistlejacket.
ALEKSANDAR HEMON, ED.,
  Best European Fiction.
AIDAN HIGGINS, *A Bestiary.*
  Balcony of Europe.
  Bornholm Night-Ferry.
  Darkling Plain: Texts for the Air.
  Flotsam and Jetsam.
  Langrishe, Go Down.
  Scenes from a Receding Past.
  Windy Arbours.
KEIZO HINO, *Isle of Dreams.*
KAZUSHI HOSAKA, *Plainsong.*
ALDOUS HUXLEY, *Antic Hay.*
  Crome Yellow.
  Point Counter Point.
  Those Barren Leaves.
  Time Must Have a Stop.
NAOYUKI II, *The Shadow of a Blue Cat.*
MIKHAIL IOSSEL AND JEFF PARKER, EDS.,
  Amerika: Russian Writers View the
  United States.
GERT JONKE, *The Distant Sound.*
  Geometric Regional Novel.
  Homage to Czerny.
  The System of Vienna.

JACQUES JOUET, *Mountain R.*
  Savage.
  Upstaged.
CHARLES JULIET, *Conversations with*
  Samuel Beckett and Bram van
  Velde.
MIEKO KANAI, *The Word Book.*
YORAM KANIUK, *Life on Sandpaper.*
HUGH KENNER, *The Counterfeiters.*
  Flaubert, Joyce and Beckett:
  The Stoic Comedians.
  Joyce's Voices.
DANILO KIŠ, *Garden, Ashes.*
  A Tomb for Boris Davidovich.
ANITA KONKKA, *A Fool's Paradise.*
GEORGE KONRÁD, *The City Builder.*
TADEUSZ KONWICKI, *A Minor Apocalypse.*
  The Polish Complex.
MENIS KOUMANDAREAS, *Koula.*
ELAINE KRAF, *The Princess of 72nd Street.*
JIM KRUSOE, *Iceland.*
EWA KURYLUK, *Century 21.*
EMILIO LASCANO TEGUI, *On Elegance*
  While Sleeping.
ERIC LAURRENT, *Do Not Touch.*
HERVÉ LE TELLIER, *The Sextine Chapel.*
  A Thousand Pearls (for a Thousand
  Pennies)
VIOLETTE LEDUC, *La Bâtarde.*
EDOUARD LEVÉ, *Suicide.*
SUZANNE JILL LEVINE, *The Subversive*
  Scribe: Translating Latin
  American Fiction.
DEBORAH LEVY, *Billy and Girl.*
  Pillow Talk in Europe and Other
  Places.
JOSÉ LEZAMA LIMA, *Paradiso.*
ROSA LIKSOM, *Dark Paradise.*
OSMAN LINS, *Avalovara.*
  The Queen of the Prisons of Greece.
ALF MAC LOCHLAINN,
  The Corpus in the Library.
  Out of Focus.
RON LOEWINSOHN, *Magnetic Field(s).*
MINA LOY, *Stories and Essays of Mina Loy.*
BRIAN LYNCH, *The Winner of Sorrow.*
D. KEITH MANO, *Take Five.*
MICHELINE AHARONIAN MARCOM,
  The Mirror in the Well.
BEN MARCUS,
  The Age of Wire and String.
WALLACE MARKFIELD,
  Teitlebaum's Window.
  To an Early Grave.
DAVID MARKSON, *Reader's Block.*
  Springer's Progress.
  Wittgenstein's Mistress.
CAROLE MASO, *AVA.*
LADISLAV MATEJKA AND KRYSTYNA
  POMORSKA, EDS.,
  Readings in Russian Poetics:
  Formalist and Structuralist Views.
HARRY MATHEWS,
  The Case of the Persevering Maltese:
  Collected Essays.
  Cigarettes.
  The Conversions.
  The Human Country: New and
  Collected Stories.
  The Journalist.

FOR A FULL LIST OF PUBLICATIONS, VISIT:
www.dalkeyarchive.com

SELECTED DALKEY ARCHIVE PAPERBACKS

My Life in CIA.
Singular Pleasures.
The Sinking of the Odradek
Stadium.
Tlooth.
20 Lines a Day.
JOSEPH MCELROY,
Night Soul and Other Stories.
THOMAS MCGONIGLE,
Going to Patchogue.
ROBERT L. MCLAUGHLIN, ED., *Innovations:*
An Anthology of
Modern & Contemporary Fiction.
ABDELWAHAB MEDDEB, *Talismano.*
HERMAN MELVILLE, *The Confidence-Man.*
AMANDA MICHALOPOULOU, *I'd Like.*
STEVEN MILLHAUSER,
The Barnum Museum.
In the Penny Arcade.
RALPH J. MILLS, JR.,
Essays on Poetry.
MOMUS, *The Book of Jokes.*
CHRISTINE MONTALBETTI, *Western.*
OLIVE MOORE, *Spleen.*
NICHOLAS MOSLEY, *Accident.*
Assassins.
Catastrophe Practice.
Children of Darkness and Light.
Experience and Religion.
God's Hazard.
The Hesperides Tree.
Hopeful Monsters.
Imago Bird.
Impossible Object.
Inventing God.
Judith.
Look at the Dark.
Natalie Natalia.
Paradoxes of Peace.
Serpent.
Time at War.
The Uses of Slime Mould:
Essays of Four Decades.
WARREN MOTTE,
Fables of the Novel: French Fiction
since 1990.
Fiction Now: The French Novel in
the 21st Century.
Oulipo: A Primer of Potential
Literature.
YVES NAVARRE, *Our Share of Time.*
Sweet Tooth.
DOROTHY NELSON, *In Night's City.*
Tar and Feathers.
ESHKOL NEVO, *Homesick.*
WILFRIDO D. NOLLEDO, *But for the Lovers.*
FLANN O'BRIEN,
At Swim-Two-Birds.
At War.
The Best of Myles.
The Dalkey Archive.
Further Cuttings.
The Hard Life.
The Poor Mouth.
The Third Policeman.
CLAUDE OLLIER, *The Mise-en-Scène.*
Wert and the Life Without End.
PATRIK OUŘEDNÍK, *Europeana.*
The Opportune Moment, 1855.
BORIS PAHOR, *Necropolis.*

FERNANDO DEL PASO,
News from the Empire.
Palinuro of Mexico.
ROBERT PINGET, *The Inquisitory.*
Mahu or The Material.
Trio.
MANUEL PUIG,
Betrayed by Rita Hayworth.
The Buenos Aires Affair.
Heartbreak Tango.
RAYMOND QUENEAU, *The Last Days.*
Odile.
Pierrot Mon Ami.
Saint Glinglin.
ANN QUIN, *Berg.*
Passages.
Three.
Tripticks.
ISHMAEL REED,
The Free-Lance Pallbearers.
The Last Days of Louisiana Red.
Ishmael Reed: The Plays.
Juice!
Reckless Eyeballing.
The Terrible Threes.
The Terrible Twos.
Yellow Back Radio Broke-Down.
JOÃO UBALDO RIBEIRO, *House of the*
Fortunate Buddhas.
JEAN RICARDOU, *Place Names.*
RAINER MARIA RILKE, *The Notebooks of*
Malte Laurids Brigge.
JULIÁN RÍOS, *The House of Ulysses.*
Larva: A Midsummer Night's Babel.
Poundemonium.
Procession of Shadows.
AUGUSTO ROA BASTOS, *I the Supreme.*
DANIËL ROBBERECHTS,
Arriving in Avignon.
JEAN ROLIN, *The Explosion of the*
Radiator Hose.
OLIVIER ROLIN, *Hotel Crystal.*
ALIX CLEO ROUBAUD, *Alix's Journal.*
JACQUES ROUBAUD, *The Form of a*
City Changes Faster, Alas, Than
the Human Heart.
The Great Fire of London.
Hortense in Exile.
Hortense Is Abducted.
The Loop.
The Plurality of Worlds of Lewis.
The Princess Hoppy.
Some Thing Black.
LEON S. ROUDIEZ, *French Fiction Revisited.*
RAYMOND ROUSSEL, *Impressions of Africa.*
VEDRANA RUDAN, *Night.*
STIG SÆTERBAKKEN, *Siamese.*
LYDIE SALVAYRE, *The Company of Ghosts.*
Everyday Life.
The Lecture.
Portrait of the Writer as a
Domesticated Animal.
The Power of Flies.
LUIS RAFAEL SÁNCHEZ,
Macho Camacho's Beat.
SEVERO SARDUY, *Cobra & Maitreya.*
NATHALIE SARRAUTE,
Do You Hear Them?
Martereau.
The Planetarium.

FOR A FULL LIST OF PUBLICATIONS, VISIT:
www.dalkeyarchive.com

SELECTED DALKEY ARCHIVE PAPERBACKS

ARNO SCHMIDT, *Collected Novellas.*
Collected Stories.
Nobodaddy's Children.
Two Novels.
ASAF SCHURR, *Motti.*
CHRISTINE SCHUTT, *Nightwork.*
GAIL SCOTT, *My Paris.*
DAMION SEARLS, *What We Were Doing*
and Where We Were Going.
JUNE AKERS SEESE,
Is This What Other Women Feel Too?
What Waiting Really Means.
BERNARD SHARE, *Inish.*
Transit.
AURELIE SHEEHAN,
Jack Kerouac Is Pregnant.
VIKTOR SHKLOVSKY, *Bowstring.*
Knight's Move.
A Sentimental Journey:
Memoirs 1917–1922.
Energy of Delusion: A Book on Plot.
Literature and Cinematography.
Theory of Prose.
Third Factory.
Zoo, or Letters Not about Love.
CLAUDE SIMON, *The Invitation.*
PIERRE SINIAC, *The Collaborators.*
JOSEF ŠKVORECKÝ, *The Engineer of*
Human Souls.
GILBERT SORRENTINO,
Aberration of Starlight.
Blue Pastoral.
Crystal Vision.
Imaginative Qualities of Actual
Things.
Mulligan Stew.
Pack of Lies.
Red the Fiend.
The Sky Changes.
Something Said.
Splendide-Hôtel.
Steelwork.
Under the Shadow.
W. M. SPACKMAN,
The Complete Fiction.
ANDRZEJ STASIUK, *Fado.*
GERTRUDE STEIN,
Lucy Church Amiably.
The Making of Americans.
A Novel of Thank You.
LARS SVENDSEN, *A Philosophy of Evil.*
PIOTR SZEWC, *Annihilation.*
GONÇALO M. TAVARES, *Jerusalem.*
Learning to Pray in the Age of
Technology.
LUCIAN DAN TEODOROVICI,
Our Circus Presents . . .
STEFAN THEMERSON, *Hobson's Island.*
The Mystery of the Sardine.
Tom Harris.
JOHN TOOMEY, *Sleepwalker.*
JEAN-PHILIPPE TOUSSAINT,
The Bathroom.
Camera.
Monsieur.
Running Away.
Self-Portrait Abroad.
Television.
DUMITRU TSEPENEAG,
Hotel Europa.

The Necessary Marriage.
Pigeon Post.
Vain Art of the Fugue.
ESTHER TUSQUETS, *Stranded.*
DUBRAVKA UGRESIC,
Lend Me Your Character.
Thank You for Not Reading.
MATI UNT, *Brecht at Night.*
Diary of a Blood Donor.
Things in the Night.
ÁLVARO URIBE AND OLIVIA SEARS, EDS.,
Best of Contemporary Mexican
Fiction.
ELOY URROZ, *Friction.*
The Obstacles.
LUISA VALENZUELA, *Dark Desires and*
the Others.
He Who Searches.
MARJA-LIISA VARTIO,
The Parson's Widow.
PAUL VERHAEGHEN, *Omega Minor.*
BORIS VIAN, *Heartsnatcher.*
LLORENÇ VILLALONGA, *The Dolls' Room.*
ORNELA VORPSI, *The Country Where No*
One Ever Dies.
AUSTRYN WAINHOUSE, *Hedyphagetica.*
PAUL WEST,
Words for a Deaf Daughter & Gala.
CURTIS WHITE,
America's Magic Mountain.
The Idea of Home.
Memories of My Father Watching TV.
Monstrous Possibility: An Invitation
to Literary Politics.
Requiem.
DIANE WILLIAMS, *Excitability:*
Selected Stories.
Romancer Erector.
DOUGLAS WOOLF, *Wall to Wall.*
Ya! & John-Juan.
JAY WRIGHT, *Polynomials and Pollen.*
The Presentable Art of Reading
Absence.
PHILIP WYLIE, *Generation of Vipers.*
MARGUERITE YOUNG, *Angel in the Forest.*
Miss MacIntosh, My Darling.
REYOUNG, *Unbabbling.*
VLADO ŽABOT, *The Succubus.*
ZORAN ŽIVKOVIĆ, *Hidden Camera.*
LOUIS ZUKOFSKY, *Collected Fiction.*
SCOTT ZWIREN, *God Head.*